Fathers day

UP ON THE
MOUNTAIN

To My Father —

May God Bless You and

Keep You Forever

Babou

Medjugorje – A Shining Inspiration

Other titles available from Paraclete Press

UP ON THE
MOUNTAIN

Father Kenneth J. Roberts

PARACLETE PRESS
Brewster, Massachusetts

In certain instances, to protect the privacy of individuals, names and dates have been changed, and some circumstances have been altered. Scripture references are taken from the New Jerusalem Bible or the New American Bible.

15 14 13 12 11 10 9 8 7

Copyright © 1992 by Kenneth J. Roberts
Library of Congress Card Number: 92-64000
All rights reserved.
Published by Paraclete Press
Brewster, Massachusetts
www.paraclete-press.com

ISBN: 1-55725-053-7
Printed in the United States of America

Author's Note

Many of my brother priests and Catholic brothers and sisters ask me why I continue to promote Medjugorje, since (as of this writing) it has not been approved by the Church. The point is, neither has it been condemned. . .

I believe that the messages of Medjugorje are authentic, because of the tremendously good fruit that has resulted from that little village. I will not say that I am absolutely certain of their authenticity; to do so would make me a fanatic, and in all things supernatural there must be an element of faith.

What if the Church condemns it? Then as a loyal priest I will never visit or mention Medjugorje again. But I would suffer no loss of faith, since the message I preach from the pulpit and in this book is the message of the gospel and the teachings of the Catholic Church.

Then why promote Medjugorje? Show me one other place on earth today, where literally millions are returning to the practice of their faith, where non-Catholics and even non-Christians are converting in great numbers, where teens who were bored with Church are going to daily Mass and spending many hours in prayer. Show me such a place—and I will go there, instead. But until you do show me such a place, I will continue to promote Medjugorje.

To those who doubt Medjugorje and its message, I would simply say: What if she really is appearing? What if this really is the last chance for the world? And for you? Have you converted?

Acknowledgements

This book would never have seen the light of day, but for God's Providence. I was attending the Christian Booksellers' annual convention last year, when by chance I met the editor of Paraclete Press, David Manuel, who suggested I write a book about Medjugorje. When I pointed out that was impossible with my busy schedule, he proposed a way it might be accomplished: he would follow me about with a tape recorder. . . .

When the working draft was ready, my schedule was busier than ever and would have kept me from doing justice to it, were it not for the aid of my good friend and recording publisher, Anna Marie Waters, the editor of Pax Tapes. Thank you both. . . . (two "eds" are better than one!)

In search of a title, three times I opened the Bible at random, and in each instance I opened to the words "up on the mountain"—first in Genesis, when Abraham was with his son Isaac; second, in Exodus, when Moses went 'up on the mountain'; lastly, in the New Testament, when Jesus was 'up on the mountain' at His Transfiguration. Thank you, Holy Spirit.

Finally, to all those who have traveled to Medjugorje— and the many more who have not, but who have heard and received the message in their hearts—again, thank you.

To all the youth who have affected my life, and allowed me to affect theirs—especially those who have answered calls to the priesthood and religious life. . .

And to all the older pilgrims, too numerous to mention, whose friendship and prayers have helped me to grow— this book is dedicated.

Contents

Foreword

If I were to "pick a word"—choose one word to best describe Father Kenneth John Roberts, it would be charismatic. His is a charisma beyond the sense of community sharing among Christians who receive and practice the gifts of the Holy Spirit; it completely embodies the personality of this English-born priest/evangelizer, which is a gratuitous gift to all who have known him.

I met Father Ken in the spring of 1987, at EWTN in Birmingham, where I had been invited to do a show with Mother Angelica about my own spiritual conversion.

Having lived a somewhat similar man-of-the-world life-style to that of Father Ken's prior to his becoming a priest, my conversion was launched by discovery and acceptance of the apparitions of the Blessed Virgin Mary at Medjugorje. It was not simply learning about the apparitions, but feeling in my heart that the Blessed Virgin had actually asked me to make the spreading of her messages given at Medjugorje my life's work. The twist was that I was a Lutheran Protestant and a newspaper journalist, who prior to learning about Medjugorje, knew nothing about the Virgin Mary or past apparitions.

On the morning of Mother's show, I attended Mass in the station's chapel; Father Ken was the celebrant. I had never heard him speak, but was aware that he was a frequent guest and speaker at EWTN, and I was sure he had never heard of me.

Within moments of the beginning of his homily, I was

mesmerized. The words of the Gospel were transformed into easily understandable parallels to everyday life. At the end of his short sermon, I was startled to hear him call my name. He was telling people about this Protestant who was here attending a Catholic Mass, because he had embraced Mary, and thus found her Son, Jesus.

Later that evening I had an opportunity to share informally with Father Ken, and was as enthralled as I had been, listening to his homily. And now, after sharing many platforms with him at Marian conferences and hearing his talks, I remain just as fascinated.

These pages adroitly capture the full charisma of Father Ken's personality which manifests itself as both prodigal son and forgiving father. His personal story takes the reader on an emotional and exciting spiritual roller-coaster ride, a conversion experience which most readers will find to some degree similar to their own, and yet unique.

Up On The Mountain brings to the reader far greater insights into the message of Medjugorje and updates in the ongoing conversion of Father Ken. These include his gradual change from so-called "intellectual" priest, to dynamic crusader for Christ through the traditional doctrines of the Roman Catholic church. His full-time evangelizing of those doctrines—especially to youth—has been further enhanced upon learning about and frequent pilgrimages to the tiny village of Medjugorje. . . .

It is simply a book to be read more than once; the charismatic personality of this dynamic man and priest almost demands it.

—*Wayne Weible*

1

3:15

The loudspeaker system crackled in the vast, high-ceilinged terminal, as the announcement came first in Croatian, then in English: due to the approach of a severe storm and high winds, the flight to New York would be delayed. The new departure time would be 3:15.

I felt the icy grip of fear in the pit of my stomach. The delay itself was not unusual; there were mountains around Zagreb, the capital of Croatia (which in the spring of '88 was still a part of former Yugoslavia), and take-offs were often held up because of high winds. No, it was the time for which our flight had been re-scheduled.

The young people among the pilgrims seemed to be hanging together; I went over to them now, and keeping my voice down in that cavernous space, I shared the reason for my concern: "There's something I have to tell you. About a month ago, I received a prophetic warning not to go on a flight that left at 3:15. It was from someone whom I am convinced was perfectly sincere. She was only trying to pass on what she believed God had given her to tell me."

I looked around at their faces—most of them young and trusting, many deeply changed by what they had experienced on our week-long pilgrimage to Medjugorje, which was now drawing to a close. They were in my charge, and I owed them this explanation. "You should also know that I received other warnings about this particular trip, from other sincere, concerned individuals. But none was quite as specific as this. Until that announcement a moment ago, I had assumed that God had other plans. Now, I am not so sure."

I looked at one, then another: "If you want to re-book on the next New York flight after this one, I am sure it can be arranged."

"Father Ken," said a button-nosed college freshman named Annie, "are you going to go on this one?"

"Yes," I replied solemnly. "I have a mission in Houston, as soon as I get back. I've got to go."

She was silent for a moment. "Well," she said thoughtfully, "if you're going, so am I."

"Me, too," said a tall football player named Bill.

"And me," added Gordon, who was studying to be a doctor.

Now the rest were nodding, too—but I held up my hand. "Look, I don't want anyone feeling pressured by the group. If even one of you would prefer to wait, that will be all right. You can come and tell me later, if you like, and we'll arrange it."

They all shook their heads. "All right, then," I smiled and looked up at the large clock on the wall. It was 10:15. "I don't know about you, but I'm going to spend most of the next five hours in prayer."

I walked over to the main entrance and looked out at the rapidly darkening sky. The temperature must have dropped ten degrees, and the first drops of rain, driven almost horizontal by the rising wind, were beginning to lash the tall windows.

They were right to keep the planes on the ground, I thought, turning back to the main hall of the terminal with a shudder. Walking back, my footsteps made a hollow, echoing sound on the marble floor. All at once I was reminded of another time when my footsteps had echoed, more than thirty years before. . . .

I was on my first flight as a new steward for BOAC (British Overseas Airways Corporation, forerunner of today's British Air)—a week-long trip to West Africa, aboard BOAC's newest airliner, the DC-7 Argonaut. After a two-day stop-over in Tripoli, we would proceed to Kano, Nigeria, for a three-day stop, then back to Tripoli and back to London. The planes themselves went straight through, but at each stop they picked up a rested flight crew. Two days before I was due to go, the dispatcher had called: "Roberts, the steward on the Argo ahead of you has taken sick. We need to move you up a flight, to take his place—that okay?"

"Uh, sure. When do we leave?"

"Tomorrow morning. Be at the ready room by 0900 hours."

"But —"

"Thanks, Roberts. Knew we could count on you." *Click.*

Parked on the tarmac awaiting its passengers, the Argo was magnificent! Inside and out, everything was gleaming and immaculate, like one of the Cunard Queens—an oceanliner of the air. In those days, the two dominant international carriers were Pan American and BOAC. There were others, heavily subsidized by the countries which ran them, but these two were the best—the Cadillac and Rolls Royce of the industry. To be a flight steward with BOAC meant travel, adventure, exotic ports of call—all the glamor that the world had to offer.

And Tripoli *was* exotic! Mosques and minarets, bazaars and boutiques—I felt like I was in a foreign film. I soon learned that while on duty, BOAC crews worked diligently and caringly like the top-flight professionals they were. But when they were off-duty, they played as hard as they worked. And I discovered something else: our company's motto— "BOAC takes good care of you!"—pertained to their flight crews, as well as their passengers. We were billeted at the best hotel, given dinner chits to the finest restaurant, and went night-clubbing at the most exclusive spots. What's more, the Chief Steward informed me, that was standard operating procedure wherever we went—Paris, Rome, Berlin, Tokyo, Hong-Kong, Cairo, Istanbul, Singapore, New York. . . .

It was an extravagant life, but with our extra pay for flying and overseas duty, plus a generous per diem allowance, we literally had more money than there was time to spend it. Jet aircraft were just beginning to replace propeller-driven planes on trans-oceanic routes, and a new phrase was being heard: "the jet set." It applied to fun-loving sophisticates who traveled to stave off boredom. We lived like them, with two exceptions: we weren't bored, and we traveled for free.

After two off-duty days in Tripoli, we reported back to the airport, to take over the flight to Cairo. We had a coffee in the lounge, then went out to the gate, to enjoy the last rays of the setting sun and watch our flight arrive.

A quick mind coupled with a quick tongue can be a mixed blessing—as my former grammar school teachers could readily attest. To see a clever comment was to speak it, and I was forever disrupting classes with uncalled-for humor. As I grew older, this behavior modified—somewhat. But it still had a tendency to surface when I was in strange circumstances or ill at ease.

Now, with a yawn I commented that if BOAC really wanted to take good care of us, they would re-schedule their Cairo flight for a more civilized hour. The younger crew members chuckled, but the senior pilot was frowning— not at my attempt at wit; at a distant billowing sand cloud about half a mile west of Runway Zero-Eight, which the Argo would be using. It was building—and coming closer.

"Damn!" he muttered. "Sand storm. I hope Roger sees it." He was looking at the far end of the runway, and there above it, about six miles out, was a tiny glint of silver. The flight from Tripoli was on time.

As it approached, so did the sand storm.

"You can set your watch by BOAC," I joked, still unaware that there was any reason for concern. This time, only the new stewardess smiled.

"Why don't you have him circle?" murmured the senior pilot, an edge to his voice. "He's got plenty of fuel." He glared at the control tower, as if willing them to realize the danger. But the Argonaut continued steadily down the glide path.

Now it was in final approach, lowering flaps and landing gear. To the left, the sand storm seemed to pick up speed, hurrying toward the end of the runway, as if late for an appointment. It almost was—the great silver plane had already touched down by the time the storm enveloped it.

"Damn!" exclaimed the senior pilot. "He's off the runway!"

"Well," I quipped, "why doesn't he get back on?" He was too caught up in his friend's desperate struggle to save his ship, to hear my inanity, but the second pilot and the navigator glanced at me with a look of revulsion.

The sand storm boiled furiously, completely obscuring the aircraft. Suddenly there was an explosion, and a ball of fire rose from its midst.

"Fuel tank!" cried the senior pilot, as he started running towards the storm. The second pilot and the navigator were right behind him, as were the older members of the crew. Then came the younger ones, including the new idiot steward.

Fire trucks and emergency vehicles had already reached the scene by the time we got there. They gave us cloths to wrap around our heads, to keep the sand out of our lungs. The plane had been broken in half by the explosion, and one wing was burning furiously. There were some survivors—a man wandering dazedly, a woman screaming and pulling at her hair, a little girl frightened out of her wits. While the fire-fighters battled the blaze, we concentrated on leading the living to safety. Then we started searching the broken fuselage—for anyone still alive, and then for bodies.

For the next three hours we labored, our navy blue uniforms turned khaki by the raging sand. And finally we had done all we could.

As we left, we passed through a deserted hangar bay, our footsteps on the concrete echoing off the corrugated steel walls. There, out of sight of the curiosity-seekers, were rows of bodies covered by navy-blue BOAC blankets. One row was shorter than the others—the flight crew, I was told. Among them was a new steward named Brad Jones. Jonesy, as we called him, had gone through training with me. He had taken my place on the Tripoli flight.

I had logged several thousand hours of flight time with BOAC after that, and far more in my current capacity as a traveling priest. I had always assumed that God had spared my life then, to do what I was presently doing, and in all that time, I had never known a moment of fear about flying—until now.

Finding an unused seat in the corner of the waiting area in the Zagreb terminal, I glanced up at the clock: it was 10:45—still a long time until 3:15. Almost a lifetime.

I bowed my head and began to pray. I knew who the author of fear—any fear—was, and I rebuked Satan and turned my thoughts to God.

Despite the warnings I had received, I had been certain that He had wanted me to come on this pilgrimage. Too many extraordinary coincidences had lined up for me to doubt it. . . .

2

A Black Cloud

It began with a call from Birmingham, Alabama. The Caritas organization was working with ABC-TV's "20/20" to put together a possible on-location feature on Medjugorje. Caritas wanted me to be the theological advisor.

"Well, it's nice of you to invite me, but I'm afraid I'm not free. March is Lent, and I'm booked for the next three years in Lent. There's no way I can get out of it."

They were persistent, arguing that I might reach a thousand people at a parish mission, but if I agreed to do "20/20", I would be reaching millions.

I conceded that, but a commitment was a commitment; I was not about to cancel out on a parish to which I had made a promise two years before. Giving Caritas the names and phone numbers of a few priests with television experience, I rang off, considering the matter closed.

Two days later, they called again: "They're all tied up, Father. You've got to reconsider."

Again I declined and gave them a few more names.

Two days later they called back: "They're all busy, too!"

But my answer remained the same; I was not about to break a promise.

According to St. Luke, after Jesus gave His disciples the "Our Father," He told them the parable of the man who went to his friend's house at midnight and knocked, because another friend, traveling from afar, had just arrived; he wanted to give him some bread. The man whom he had awakened said no, but the man at the door kept on knocking, until finally his friend opened the door and gave him the bread he had requested.

The Caritas people must have memorized that passage. They called one more time: "We believe the Lord wants you to do this. We've all prayed about it, our prayer team has prayed about it, and we're getting confirmation from all over the country: Father Roberts is the one who's supposed to go!"

I refrained from giving my standard reply to that approach: as soon as God tells me the same thing that He has apparently told you. . . . But finally I did say that if God wanted me to go, He would have to make it possible.

And so one morning, as I was saying Mass in my own parish, I asked the children at Mass to pray for a special intention. I did not tell them what it was, but it was to Mary: if she wanted me to go, she would have to make something happen.

When I got back to the rectory after that Mass, my secretary said, "Father, you've just had a request for a cancellation."

"Really? When?"

"In March." She gave me the message, and I called them.

"Father," said the pastor, a trifle embarrassed, "Would

you mind if we canceled your mission? The bishop has just informed me that he would be delighted to come for confirmation and—well, it will be quite a clash to have the confirmation and the mission going on at the same time. . . Could we possibly re-schedule you for another time?"

So there it was. Actually it was two weeks after 20/20 was going, but I called another parish and asked them if they would mind delaying my mission to them for two weeks, to free up the week in question. "Father, we'd love it!" they responded. "To tell you the truth, it's a much better week for us!"

I was chuckling when I hung up. I would have to tell our children how strong their prayers were: in half an hour the Blessed Mother had arranged what I had repeatedly been saying day after day was impossible!

The Caritas people were elated, and I was off on my next mission, to a beautiful church in Omaha, Nebraska. As it happened, the pastor there appreciated good cooking and had gone to considerable trouble to find a real chef for a cook. He had located one—a woman who much preferred to prepare dinner for three priests, instead of for a restaurant full of people.

One evening after a sumptuous repast, I went into the kitchen to get a cup of tea. Startled, the chef backed away from me. I was a bit startled myself; I didn't usually have that effect on people. Then I realized that she wasn't used to talking to priests.

"Don't be put off by this," I said, gesturing to my clerical collar. "I'm really quite harmless."

"I'm not Catholic," she said warily. "I work for the priests, but I don't talk to them. I'm Assembly of God," she added, as if that explained everything.

It did—and it didn't. I had met other Christians who, like her, were more comfortable keeping high walls between themselves and others. I enjoyed talking over the walls to them, and often, they enjoyed the conversation, too. Before they knew it, the wall between us had diminished to the point of insignificance.

So now, instead of leaving when she handed me the cup of tea she had made for me, I continued chatting. "How long have you worked here?"

"A couple of years, but I don't have anything to do with them," she nodded toward the dining room. "I just cook the meal, and they wheel it in, and that's it."

"Do you know anything about Catholicism?" I asked, smiling.

She shook her head. "I worship Jesus, the Lord," she said emphatically.

"So do I."

She looked at me, frowning. "You mean, Jesus is your Saviour?"

"Of course!"

"But I thought you all worshipped Mary." She was becoming more interested than cautious.

"No, no," I laughed, "we worship Jesus, the Lord. We love His mother, but we worship the Lord."

When I did leave the kitchen that evening, the wall between us was much lower.

Every night for the rest of my mission, I went back for another cup of tea, and we would sit at the kitchen table and chat. We became friends, and as friends who love the Lord often do, we prayed together. The wall was still there, and we stayed on our respective sides of it. But it was little more than a ridge in the sand. Praying together at the foot of the Cross, we were one.

On my last day there, when I went to say good-bye to my new-old friend, she was sad that I was leaving. I sensed there was something she wanted to say.

"Father, I hate to ask you this, but I have the gift of the word of knowledge." She hesitated. "Could I pray with you, with that gift? Would you find that offensive?"

"No," I assured her, smiling. "I would be honored."

So she took my hands in hers to pray with me—and then immediately she took them off and put them to her mouth. "Father!" she said, her eyes widening. "Are you flying overseas in the next month?"

"Yes, why?"

"Don't fly on a plane that leaves at 3:15!"

"How come?"

"I don't know what it means, but I just saw the word 'crash', and I heard a crash, and I saw the numbers 3:15."

"I'll certainly try not to," I said, trying to placate her as best I could.

I tried to dismiss the incident as a harmless eccentricity, but as soon as I got back to my office, I checked the flight schedule for our forthcoming trip to Medjugorje. It didn't matter, of course, I told myself—and was more than a little relieved to find that none of our flights was scheduled for a 3:15 departure.

My next mission was in New Orleans, and I went down early, to have some time off before it began. When I learned that Father Mike Scanlan and Sister Briege McKenna were in town and giving a day of renewal, I wound up taking a busman's holiday. Seeing me in the audience, they invited me up to the sanctuary and then to go to a friend's home, to have lunch with them.

"You know," I confided, "the strangest thing happened to me out in Omaha," and I told them the story.

When I finished, Briege matter-of-factly announced: "We'll pray with you," as if that would resolve everything.

They did—and it didn't; in fact, in a way it compounded my dilemma. When we had returned to the chapel, after they had prayed for me, Briege said: "I don't know what this means, but as we were praying, I saw a black cloud over you. You were in a field, and it looked like Medjugorje, but I can't be sure."

"What does it mean?" I asked, now more worried than I had been before.

She shrugged and smiled. "I only get these visions; I don't interpret them."

I did not smile back. I knew how accurate Briege McKenna's visions could be. It was she who had seen the fountains of living water which had foretold the coming of the Blessed Mother to Medjugorje.

I did not share my own interpretation of the black cloud: taken with the word about the crash, I took it to be a sign of death.

Which left me in a fine state, as there were now less than two weeks before I would fly down to Birmingham, to pick up the group of young people being sponsored by Caritas. As it happened, I went down sooner than that: Mother Angelica sent for me.

It was good to see this cheery soul who had become a close friend over the years—but I was surprised to see Father Mike McDonough, my spiritual director, whom she had apparently also sent for. After our greetings, she called Anna Marie Schmidt, a mystic who was also a regular on EWTN. Originally from Czechoslovakia, her family had been killed during the war, and she had been held in a concentration camp by the Germans and then by the Russians. She was very holy, and the Lord spoke to her.

She was also a very solid person, and I respected her.

Mother Angelica handed me the phone. "Father," Anna Marie explained, "I don't want to discourage you or worry you, but Mother asked me to pray for the success of your trip to Medjugorje. I don't know what it means, but every time I pray for someone, and there's danger or a warning, I get a chilled spine."

"And —?"

But she would not be hurried. "I warned Father Bertolucci not to go to Hong Kong, because I had gotten a tingling in my spine. He didn't listen to me, and you know what happened: he fell off that pier and broke his leg." She then told me of another priest who had not heeded her warning; he had actually gotten killed.

Her voice took on a solemnity: "Father, I never had such a frozen spine, as when I prayed for you."

"What do you think it means?" I managed to ask.

"I don't know what it means; I'm just passing on the message: when I prayed for you my spine was frozen."

I was nonplussed. I thanked her, and when I had hung up, Mother asked, "What are you going to do?"

I looked at the back of my hands, then up at her. "I don't see as I have a choice. When I make a commitment, I keep it. And I've told them I would come."

Now Father Mike spoke: "Ken, don't put yourself in jeopardy. The Church needs you."

"Does God know that?" I asked him.

"Yes."

"Then God will protect us."

He smiled and shook his head. "You know, God also gives us signs. . ." And he reminded me of the story about the man trapped on his rooftop by a sudden flood.

I knew the story: A man in a rowboat came by and

offered to take him to safety, but the man on the roof declined the offer. "I've asked God to save me, and I have every confidence that He will soon abate this flood."

The water level rose; it was now almost to the peak of the roof. Another boat came by, this one a rescue craft with paramedics aboard. Again, the man on the roof declined their offer. "God will save me; my faith in that is stronger than ever. You'll see: any minute now, the waters will start receding."

But they didn't; they rose higher, until the man was standing on the peak of his house, with only his head above water. But his faith was unflagging. When a helicopter spotted him and started to lower a ladder, he waved it off, shouting: "Don't worry about me; God is going to save me!"

The waters rose still higher, and the man eventually drowned. When he stood before his Creator, he demanded to know why God had not answered his prayers. "But I did," replied God. "I sent you two boats and a helicopter."

Father Mike now looked at me smiled. "Ken," he said gently, "I think God has sent you two boats and a helicopter!"

By now I believed that I was going to be killed—but I had a deep peace about it. Because I also believed that it was God's will for me to go. Being a priest, it was a relatively simple thing for me to put my affairs in order. Nor was I shaken, when my secretary told me that she, too, had a bad feeling about this trip and wished I wouldn't go. By the time we were due to leave, I was really convinced I had one week to live.

To sharpen the focus on their spiritual priorities, I had often asked people: "If you knew for sure you only had one week left to live, how would you live it?"

I was about to find out what my own answer would be.

3

Edge of Heaven

The Zagreb terminal clock said 11:10; there were still four hours to wait. My thoughts went back to a week ago, as we were preparing for this pilgrimage. Could it have been only a week? It seemed more like a year. . . .

If I had a week to live, what would I do? Would I spend it in prayer? Would I go see all the people I wanted to say good-bye to? Would I go to a monastery? Would I stay in church all day? What *would* I do?

I didn't know. And I thought I never would. But now that I really believed I had only one week left, I didn't change anything.

I *was* much more aware of everything—of colors and music and textures and aromas. Of memories, and the places my mind went, when it was not occupied. Of the nuances of other people's feelings, little things which I had not picked up before.

And my prayer times were wonderful! Since I expected to be with Him soon, I went into them at peace—and came

16

out serene. I came into a new depth of understanding of what it meant simply to commune with God. And, I discovered, it was possible to extend that communion, that sense of His intimate presence, even as I went about the tasks of daily living. So *this* was what it meant, to pray without ceasing. . . .

I was no saint, of course. I could not sustain it indefinitely. It was possible—but I allowed myself to be distracted by the cares of the world. Still, whenever I entered the inner prayer room of my heart and shut the door, I was alone with Him—and was content to remain there, as long as He desired.

People who knew of the warnings I had received, could not understand how I could be so tranquil. Some were even a little annoyed; it was unnatural. "What if you do get killed?"

"Well—I'm ready. And what better way to go than in Mary's service?"

Anyway, I knew it wasn't going to be the flight over, which left New York at 9:00 PM. My peace *was* disturbed a little bit, because Heart of the Nation, hearing that I was going over as a theological advisor and narrator for 20/20, decided that they wanted to do a documentary also, and asked me if I would help. I said sure, as long as what they wanted to do didn't conflict with my 20/20 obligations. But that was the trouble: neither crew thought they were going to get enough footage with me, as long as the other one was around.

The flight over was uneventful, and I settled back to pray.

Recently a friend asked me: "How do you do it?"

"Do what?"

"Keep going at that pace? Father Ken, you'd exhaust

the Energizer Bunny! You seem to have your switch thrown to 'on' *all* the time—how do keep from burning out?"

"I don't burn out, because I refuel. The Blessed Mother asked us to pray three hours a day—you'd be amazed how much that revitalizes you!" As long as I spent at least as much time in solitary prayer, as I did saying Mass or talking to groups, my well did not run dry. And since I was giving talks and celebrating Mass practically every day and sometimes three or four times a day, that meant a lot of time in that inner prayer room.

With spiritual equilibrium restored, I thought ahead to Medjugorje—and found my heart rejoicing at the thought of returning to that remote, rustic setting, high in the mountains of Hercegovina. I wondered if the breathtaking beauty of that little valley nestled among the mountains, as in the hollow of God's hand, was merely natural? Or was it under a special heavenly grace, because the Mother of God had been re-appearing there every day for seven years?

This was my third pilgrimage, and despite the dire prophecies, I was more anxious to get back than ever. I smiled at that thought, because on my first, in the summer of '86, I hadn't particularly wanted to go; in fact, I was sort of railroaded into it.

Like this one, it had begun in Birmingham. I was flying in to do a talk show with Mother Angelica on EWTN, and at the airport, I passed a well-dressed gentleman who said hello. Because of all the TV exposure, that happened to me a lot, but I thought I recognized this man's face, though I couldn't place his name. Well, he was catching a plane, and I had just landed, so I didn't think any more about it.

That night on the show, a woman called in with a

question: "Mother Angelica, have you ever heard of Medjugorje?"

"Oh, yes."

"Is it all right to go there, Mother?"

"Yes," she said smiling, "you go there, honey, and pray for me."

But I was more cautious. The Church had not yet approved of Medjugorje, and how could we be certain it was genuine?

Mother Angelica and I had worked together for a long time, and she was quite sensitive to what I was feeling, even if I didn't say anything. Now she picked up my unspoken hesitation, and being in a mischievous mood, she turned to me and said, "Would you like to go there, Father?"

"Not particularly."

Then she turned to the camera and said, beaming: "Father Roberts will go there, and he'll tell us all about it."

So that was the end of that!

When the show was over, I went back to the guest house where I was staying, and to my surprise the man from the airport was there. He was laughing. "I just saw the show," he said, "and now I know why God had me miss that plane. It's your fault."

"Pardon?"

He held out a hand. "I'm John Haffert. I'm the one who's going to send you to Medjugorje."

I shook his hand. I knew who he was now: the founder of the Blue Army. "You're—going to send me there?"

He nodded. "We'll put the Blue Army's 707 at your disposal."

"Well, that's very nice of you," I smiled, "but I don't

have any time off; I'm booked solidly for two years." Which I would explain to Mother Angelica, as soon as I had the chance.

But John Haffert was cut from the same bolt of cloth; he just didn't seem to understand that other people might have schedules that precluded. . . .

"Let's get your calendar out."

So I opened up my calendar, and in all of 1986, I had one block of eight days open, in July.

"That's perfect!" he cried. "We'll do a trip of eight days. We'll go to Rome first, then Medjugorje, and then Fatima."

"We're going to go all those places in eight days?" I said 'we' before I realized that I was agreeing to go.

"No problem; we've got our own plane, remember."

"How on earth are you going to fill it?"

"No problem there, either. All we have to do is put the word out, and there'll be a waiting list!"

And there was. Suddenly there was this giant group of people with us, six busloads full, and we had a great time leading them around Rome. Then we went to Dubrovnik, and up to Medjugorje for one day, appropriately the Fourth of July. We arrived in time for the English Mass, which I was invited to celebrate.

I loved St. James Church! The prayers of several million pilgrims seemed to have left a sacred residue on the very rafters, making it that much more easy to pray there. It was a holy place, and yet also a cozy one, if the word could be used for such a large church. And it was an inviting place; you couldn't help smiling as you entered the large front portals.

The only people not smiling were our two Communist guides. Back then, the Communist government had not yet realized what a hard-currency boon Medjugorje was, and being a system founded on atheism, they barely tolerated its existence. Their attitude was one of thinly-veiled condescension, for if God did not exist, then all these people coming because a few children claimed to be daily seeing His mother were pathetically deluded. They would harass them at every opportunity, confiscating rosaries and Bibles at the airport, and buzzing the church with their helicopters during Mass.

In a couple of years, of course, someone in the upper echelons of the government hierarchy woke up, and the policy was reversed; now the Communists began building new pilgrim accommodations as fast as the villagers themselves were. And you could always tell which belonged to the Communists: they were the ones where the workers kept at it on Sundays.

All right, I thought on the Fourth of July, it was America's national birthday, and I knew just the hymn I was going to have them sing. As the Mass ended, I started it: "Mine eyes have seen the glory of the coming of the Lord. . ."

From that time on, *The Battle Hymn of the Republic,* sung in Croatian, became an extremely popular hymn in Medjugorje—and I've even heard that the Blessed Mother has said it's her favorite.

In America, many Medjugorje centers grew out of that trip—including some Medjugorje works which would become nationally known.

In one day, of course—just a few hours, actually, you cannot begin to experience Medjugorje. But I had seen enough to want to come back. God was definitely doing something there, and never had I seen a place where people so readily opened their hearts to Him. I was aware of literally hundreds of hearts turning to Him or back to Him, and I could feel the prayer going on around me. Before I left,

I knew I would be coming back as soon as my schedule permitted. And I was going to do something about that schedule. . . .

My second pilgrimage took place a year and a month later, in August of '87. I took eighty-eight young people, high-school seniors and college students, from many U.S. cities. This time, we had a whole week, the traditional length for a pilgrimage there—which is barely enough time to do everything one wants to do. We went up Podbrdo (Apparition Hill) and saw where the Blessed Mother first appeared, and where she would still occasionally come to open-air gatherings late at night. It was a barren, rocky, open space, and there were candle stubs and little crosses everywhere. We had some quiet time, and as with so many locations in Medjugorje, it was awfully easy to pray there.

On our second day, we met with the visionary, Vicka, on the terrace of her home. Here everyone had a chance to ask the questions that they longed to—what kind of clothes did the Blessed mother wear, what color were her eyes, and so on. I marveled at Vicka—she answered each question with patience and enthusiasm, as if she had never heard it before. In front of her house, waiting their turn with her, was a group of pilgrims from the Philippines, and behind them a group of Italians, and behind them a group from Ireland. . . . Yet in her voice, in her expressions and gestures, there was not a trace of weariness or boredom. On the contrary, her caring concern for the pilgrims was remarkable!

To people who say, "How can you tell if Medjugorje is of God?" I say, "Judge the tree by its fruit." As the Lord said, "A sound tree cannot bear bad fruit, nor a rotten tree bear good fruit" (Matt. 7:18). Looking at Vicka, giving and giving of herself for no reward but the knowledge that she was pleasing God, I would say that, if Vicka is a sample of the fruit of Medjugorje, it is hard to imagine a tree more sound.

On our third day, we climbed Mount Krizevac. The large mountain to the south of the village had a massive cement cross on its summit which was visible for miles. it was a rocky climb, not too steep but rugged, nonetheless, though the jagged edges on the path had been worn smooth by the soles of several million pairs of shoes and sandals. An Italian sculptor had created some magnificent depictions on bronze tablets of the various scenes of the Passion for the Stations of the Cross, and we stopped and prayed and meditated at each of these on our way up.

The view from the top was spectacular. You could see the red-tiled houses below, clustered around the twin-spired church like chicks around a mother hen. Over to the right was the hamlet of Bijacovici, where the visionaries Vicka and Marija lived, and above their houses, Apparition Hill, where we had been two days before. Straight ahead in the distance, you could see where the River Neretva ran, though you couldn't actually see it, and beyond it were a range of mountains higher than the one on which we stood, anchored on the right by the vast, brooding presence of snow-capped Mount Velez.

And of course, each evening, before the Croatian Mass, we would gather in the courtyard outside the rectory, to say the rosary, while inside, around 5:40 PM, the Blessed Mother appeared to at least one of the visionaries. You knew she was there, because abruptly the rosary ceased, and there was just silence.

One afternoon I was invited by Father Slavko Barbaric,

the visionaries' spiritual director, to come inside and be present for an apparition. The room, which the rest of the time was his office, was packed. Ivan came in, and we knelt and started the rosary. All at once he stopped, and we stopped. I looked where his gaze was transfixed, but I saw nothing. Nor had I heard of anyone else who had seen her, although there are more than a few photographs circulating which purport to have been snapped at this moment.

How, then, can you be certain that she actually is there? You can't. As at Fatima and Lourdes, there is an element of faith involved. But I keep going back to the fruit and the tree: God has called us to be fruit inspectors. And on my first real pilgrimage to that place, I could see the fruit of Medjugorje in the young people who had accompanied me.

For many, it began as a case of acute sensory deprivation—the first time in their lives that they had been without music or television, cars or telephones, radios or newspapers—all the world's myriad distractions and entertainments. For an entire week, there was only themselves and God, in that isolated, simple place.

One of the things I especially like about working with young people is the combination of honesty and idealism I find in them. They want absolutes. And they have not yet been conditioned to accept compromise.

Jesus is the only absolute I know of, which has never disappointed them. Confronted with His reality. . . and His love. . . and His call. . . they have no choice but to give their lives to Him, absolutely.

The great thing about young people is, they are not afraid of absolutes. Once they know in their hearts that it is truth, they can make the commitment—even if it costs them their lives.

And that week, many did. You could actually see them re-arranging their priorities. The things of God became increasingly important to them; the things of the world diminished and receded until many wanted only to remain in God's presence—happy to go wherever He directed them, happy to do whatever He called them to do.

Indeed, when it finally came time to leave Medjugorje, many of my young charges were saddened. "Father Ken," said one girl, "this doesn't make any sense! Here I am, crying about leaving this place, and yet I've got a family at home who loves me, and I love them, and I can't wait to get home to see them!"

All I could do that first trip was nod and put an arm around her; I felt the same way.

Later, after many trips to that place, I could offer an explanation. Medjugorje has been called "the edge of heaven," and in a sense that's true: the pilgrim receives a foretaste of what it will be like to spend eternity in God's presence. His (or her) spirit unites with God's, and remains there, like a nesting bird. All its life, it has been searching for this communion, this oneness, and now it has found it!

But the soul is saying that it is time to return—to the world, the old life, all the cares and responsibilities that were still there. And the spirit grieves. It cannot bear the prospect of being torn away from this sublime reunion.

What the young pilgrim does not realize, of course, and what I gently tell them, is: you can take Medjugorje with you. You can have this oneness with God at home. You will have to work at it. You will have to discipline yourself to enter the prayer room of your heart often. You will have to defend your quiet times as a lioness would her cubs. But it can be done. You can do it.

On our next to last day there, some of the girls in our

group came to me and said, "Father Ken, did you know that Jack hasn't made his First Communion?"

"He hasn't?" I was surprised; Jack was nineteen. "Why did he come on this trip?"

One of the girls laughed. "His girlfriend asked him to come."

I went to Jack and asked him if he would like to make his first Communion while we were here. His eyes brightened at the possibility. "I would, Father," he said solemnly, and that night by way of preparation, he spent the whole night up on Mount Krizevac in prayer.

The following evening, our last, we gathered under the stars in a little courtyard at the foot of Apparition Hill. It was a very special occasion, as such sharing times at the end of pilgrimages or retreats often are. One by one, they took turns sharing what the pilgrimage had meant to them, and how their lives would be different, as a result. One testimony seemed to confirm the next, and there were many tears. But perhaps the most moving was that of the young man who had come on the trip with a punk hairdo. Now he had washed it out and asked someone to give him a haircut; he looked positively radiant.

At the head of the table sat Jack, and around him the girls set and lit candles which they had obtained as a surprise. The night was warm, a gentle breeze stirred a nearby grapevine, and the stars were bright. But none was brighter than the light in Jack's eyes, as he made his confession and then received the Holy Eucharist.

That blessed ending to my second pilgrimage could not have been better preparation for the third. In fact, it offered the right spiritual balance for my pervading sense of imminent demise.

4

Two Down. . .

The airplane's loudspeaker informed us that it was time to return our trays and seat-backs to their upright positions. The first leg of my third pilgrimage—this pilgrimage—was nearly over. One long bus-ride, and we would be there. I could hardly wait—and the best part about bringing new people to Medjugorje, was to watch the effect that the village had on them.

No matter how much they already knew about the place or how many books they'd read, nothing could prepare them for what they were going to find.

In the summer of 1981, it was just another village in the mountains of the province of Hercegovina which comprised the lower half of Bosnia-Hercegovina, one of the six republics making up the nation of Yugoslavia (which meant "Kingdom of the South Slavs"). For hundreds of years this region had been devoutly Catholic, thanks to the missionary work of the Franciscans during the Fourteenth Century.

During the four hundred-year occupation of the Ottoman Turks, there had been intense persecution, as the Turks tried to crush the Church, but the Franciscans did not abandon their flocks. They hid in the mountains and continued to administer the Sacraments. Many were martyred as a result, but the people never forgot their courage.

But something *was* different about Medjugorje—something that set this little village apart. There was a deep, abiding faith in the *Gospa* (the Blessed Mother) here. When the crops—tobacco and grapes, mostly—were failing, the women of the village undertook to erect a huge cement cross on the summit of Mount Krizevac in 1933, to commemorate the nineteen-hundredth anniversary of the Crucifixion. The men carried up the materials that would be necessary, but it was the women who initiated the project. Not too surprisingly, the valley's crops flourished thereafter.

In 1953, the villagers made another significant act of faith; they built a new church—three times as large as could possibly be justified by the number of parishioners (about four hundred families). Despite the seeming illogic of it, or the extravagant cost, they were obedient to the leading of God.

It was this faith and this obedience that may have caused the most faithful and most obedient mortal who ever lived, to appear in this place. In any event, late in the afternoon of June 24, 1981, two teen-age girls from the village were out for a walk, when one saw a shining figure on a hill behind their hamlet of Bijacovici. Intuitively, she knew it was the *Gospa*. Her friend thought she was kidding—until she saw it, too.

Shaken, they ran to get some friends—who also saw this figure of a woman holding an infant in her arms. The next day, six of them returned, and saw the same shining figure. And these were the six young people to whom she would continue to appear, day after day.

Needless to say, the local Communists were in a quandary. One of the foundation stones of the Communist system was that God did not exist. How then were they to deal with the phenomenon of local young people purporting to see the apparition of the woman who gave birth to His Son? If God did not exist, He could not very well have had an earthly mother.

On the other hand, the people of the Balkans were known for their hot-bloodedness and the tenacity of their faith. Wisely, Tito had adopted a policy of tolerance towards Christianity—and Islam, too, for that matter. Let them have their religion—only restrict it to certain times and certain places, and discourage it socially. Then start training the school-children to be good Communists; in two generations there would be no more problem.

But now there was a considerable problem: their informers were reporting that hundreds of local people were flocking to that hillside in Medjugorje each afternoon, where the young people allegedly saw their vision. Soon the concern of the Communists apparatchiks deepened to alarm, as the number of onlookers swelled to several thousand, with people driving from as far away as Mostar (according to their license plates), to be there.

Something had to be done quickly, or they would be hearing from Sarajevo or even Belgrade. They called in the pastor of the parish of Medjugorje, Father Jozo Zovko, and articulated their concern. He shared it. He himself had just returned from an errand of mercy and was appalled to find out what had been taking place in his absence.

But later, as Father Jozo prayed about what to do, he, too, was given to see the Blessed Mother and was warned to protect the children. This he did—and ultimately wound up spending a year and a half in prison, because he refused to denounce them or cooperate with the authorities.

(I am giving a greatly-truncated summary here. It is a truly enthralling story, one of the great spiritual adventures of our time, or any time—and one that has been told extremely well by others. If you haven't read of it, and would like to, there are a number of titles in a bibliography at the back. The one that continues to be the most popular is by the friend who has written the foreword to this book, Wayne Weible.)

The authorities next tried to discredit the visionaries, as they were now being called, by sending a state psychiatrist out to the hillside, to investigate. She did—and then quit her position and moved away. At police headquarters, they interrogated the young people, Communist-style, but they could not break their stories. And when in frustration they took the six to the state clinic in Mostar, instead of the doctors declaring them insane and giving them an excuse to commit them, they pronounced the six young people normal, healthy, and well-balanced!

Because the Communists had never successfully subdued the people of Hercegovina and therefore (rightly) feared a spontaneous popular uprising against their regime, all mass meetings were strictly against the law. So far, the gatherings over in Medjugorje had been peaceful and non-political, but. . .

They issued an edict: if these six were going to continue making fools of themselves and those whom they were so easily impressing, they would have to do so in the church. Henceforth, there would be no more open-air gatherings.

And then the pilgrims started to come. From Italy, at first, and then from Ireland and the U.K., and the

Philippines—wherever the Catholic faith was strong. The Americans did not start coming in significant numbers until after Fathers Mike Scanlan and John Bertolucci came over in 1984, to see for themselves. But then they did come, and they told their friends. . . .

At first, the Government made it extremely difficult for the pilgrims, but gradually, as they persisted in coming— and spending considerable foreign currency—the Communists went back to their stance of disdainful tolerance.

Why did so many want to go to Medjugorje? They could not imagine. And, frankly, neither could I—until I had come to see for myself. Now, one of my greatest enjoyments was watching others discover what I had discovered.

Their first reaction was usually shock—at how rustic and inaccessible the place was. "Father, this really is the boonies!" was the response of more than one. And it was true: whoever first coined that expression would have a new definition of boondocks, once they had come to Medjugorje.

Goats were still herded down the streets of the village. Many of the roads were still unpaved, and paths across fields were often the best way to get from A to B. Barnyard aromas were the prevailing fragrance, and people still loaded hay on horse-drawn wagons with the three-pronged wooden forks used by their great-grandfathers.

Why did the Blessed Mother come to such a primitive place? Well, when she first introduced her Son to the world, it was in a lowly stable. Was it not fitting that, to re-introduce her Son to the world, she would pick as humble and primitive a setting?

After they got done wrinkling their noses, the next thing our new young pilgrims discovered was the lack of modern facilities. Pilgrims were traditionally housed in the homes of the local villagers, and these homes were not equipped with central heating. Nor did they have much hot water, so showers were brief and infrequent.

What was more, there were no radios in their rooms to hear music, no television sets, nothing to read, and usually only one telephone in the house. The phone system (which was more inexplicably unreliable than any country I had ever been to), was also exorbitantly expensive. For someone my age, all of the above could add up to heaven. But for a young person, it could result in acute withdrawal symptoms.

When you give something up, however—and let's face it, we're talking about what amounts to a rather severe fast here—God usually provides some strong positives to take its place. In Medjugorje, there was so much grace that just about everything that happened to one, wound up having fairly deep spiritual meaning.

And so, the young pilgrims became comfortable experiencing the presence of God. And the more they did, the softer their features would become. Young men who initially spouted sarcastic banter to cover their insecurity, would quiet down and become unafraid of showing sensitivity. Young women who came pre-occupied with their hair or their clothes or whether the young men were paying sufficient attention, found their concern shifting to pleasing their Lord. It was a miraculous transformation, and one that I would never grow tired of observing.

As the plane banked to line up on its glide path, I noted the snow on the mountains and wondered how cold it would be in Medjugorje, which was now only hours away.

Medjugorje, when we got there, was very cold. In fact, it was the coldest March in the villagers' recent memory.

It was certainly the coldest I had ever been—in any month, or any country! In the house where we were billeted, each room had one of those little oil heaters in it, which could not burn your hand if you put it right on one.

That first night I donned just about every garment I had brought with me—pajamas, shirts, sweater, bathrobe. It didn't help—all night long, my teeth chattered uncontrollably. And my spine was frozen. All of a sudden, I burst out laughing: Anna Marie, I think I've found your frozen spine! Only it's not yours, it's mine!

The next day we met with the visionary, Vicka, out in a field, and if you've seen the 20/20 documentary, that's the part where Vicka prays for the young man, who then breaks down and cries. In that scene, you can see how dark the sky is above us—but it is not nearly so striking on the screen, as it was that day out in the field. Everyone was pointing up: "Father, look at how black that cloud is over us!"

They were alarmed—but I was laughing: Briege McKenna, I think we've found your cloud!

Two down, one to go.

But that last one was a killer. . . .

5

Head Over Heels

At the same time I was working for 20/20, I had also agreed to do two shows for Heart of the Nation, and the 20/20 crew was irritated; they didn't want the Heart of the Nation crew hanging around them, or riding in on their coattails. So the two crews could not be together, and now each crew was claiming my allegiance.

I needed the wisdom of Solomon—and I came up with a Solomonic solution: I would split myself. I would give Heart of the Nation one full day, during which 20/20 could shoot cut-away footage, of mountains, farmers, vineyards, services, and so on. At first, Heart of the Nation did not think they could get enough usable footage in just one day, but I assured them that in the twenty-six-week series I had done for EWTN, we sometimes shot five or even six shows a day, back to back—and hardly ever had to do a retake.

The trouble was, the day we picked was a blustery one, and the noise of the wind across the microphones made it impossible to shoot out of doors. But where to shoot indoors? St. James was about the only enclosed space large enough, and someone suggested that I could do two teachings from the choir loft, speaking to the rest of our group, gathered below in the pews.

To do this, of course, we would have to obtain permission from the pastor, Father Tomislav Pervan. But as it turned out, this was not a problem; the priests, as well as the villagers, were happy to cooperate with any media group sincerely interested in promulgating the message of Medjugorje.

We started early in the afternoon, well ahead of the time for the rosary, so that there would be no conflict. The choir loft was actually quite small—there was enough room for me and the camera crew, but not a whole lot more.

My first talk was on faith and trust. I was reading from Matthew (6:25) where Jesus told His followers not to worry about what they would eat, or what they would drink; pagans worried about such things. He told them to look at the example of the lilies of the field, and so on.

"In other words," I said, looking at our friends below, "what He's saying is: trust Me. And trust is more than just believing; trust is putting faith into action."

I smiled at a sudden recollection. "You know, the first time I taught on this was to some kids in Sunday School. I said to a young boy: 'Do you trust me?' And he said, 'Sure!' And I said, 'Do you believe in me?' 'Uh-huh.' They were quick answers that didn't cost him anything. But then I said, 'I'm going to give you a chance to prove it.' And I had him stand with his back to me. 'Now fall over backwards; don't worry, I'll catch you.' But he didn't move. 'I thought you said you trusted me.' 'Not that much,' came the quick reply.

The people in the pews laughed. They could see the scene I was painting. But there was a nervousness to their laughter; they were putting themselves in the place of that boy and wondering if they would be that trusting.

To make them feel better, I added: "I tried a second boy, who assured me that, unlike his friend, he *would* trust me. But when it came to the moment of truth, he, too, balked. I had to try three more boys, before I found one who really did trust me enough to fall backwards into my waiting arms."

I looked at our friends below. They had gotten the message. I underlined it anyway: "We tell God we trust Him. And we believe it. And we *do*—up to a point. But when it comes time to let go and fall backwards—and trust that He will be there for us, that's when it gets hard."

I looked at one upturned face after another. "Are *you* willing to fall over backwards? This very afternoon?" And I left them with that thought.

My second talk would be on the Magnificat. And here was a curious tie-in with Briege McKenna's vision. For the home where we had lunch that day when she saw the black cloud, belonged to the lady who founded Magnificat, the Catholic counterpart to the Protestant Charismatics' organization, Women Aglow. When she heard that I was going to be doing some shows for Heart of the Nation, she asked me if I might mention their organization, and I said I would be happy to.

The only way to do that, was to talk on Mary's Magnificat. But what better place on earth to address that subject, and what better time, than in the choir loft of St. James Church in Medjugorje, shortly before the Blessed Mother herself would be appearing there?

The heart of my talk on the Magnificat was that Mary is like a magnifying glass: You don't look *at* a magnifying glass; you look *through* it.

"Or, if you haven't looked through a magnifying glass lately," I told them, "think of eye-glasses: no matter how beautiful your eye-glasses are—and you might have the most gorgeous pair of designer glasses—you don't look at them; you look through them."

I reminded them of Mary's response to Elizabeth, when the latter, filled with the Holy Spirit of God, was given the wisdom to recognize the magnitude of Mary's calling. "In that instant of revelation," I exclaimed, looking down at them, "Elizabeth *knew* that her kinswoman would be blessed among all women, and she *knew* who was in Mary's womb!"

For a moment I was speechless at the thought that in a few minutes we would all be repeating those very words of Elizabeth—with Mary! Right here, where I was standing!

Collecting myself, I added: "But what was Mary's response? 'My soul doth magnify the Lord!' She knew that she was merely a magnifying glass. 'Don't look at me,' she said then—as she has been saying ever since—'look *through* me, to Jesus!' Which really sums up what Mary is all about in Catholic devotion."

I recalled for them, the example that St. Francis of Assisi had given: "Think of the sun as Christ. All that the moon (Mary) does is reflect the light of Christ. The moon has no light of its own; it's only role is to reflect and magnify the light of the sun."

At the end of my talk on the Magnificat, I gave a little plug for the organization of the same name, telling people whom to contact, if they wanted to start a chapter in their home town.

When the red light on the camera blinked off, our producer, Barbara Valentine, was seeing red. She was furious! "Father, we're going to have to do that again!"

"Why?"

"You just gave a commercial!"

"Well, it was only a little one."

She didn't smile. "Father, we cannot give commercials in the show; we can't promote things."

"Why not? It's spiritual."

"If we do that, we're going to have to do it for Cursillo, Marriage Encounter, the Charismatic Renewal, the Legion of Mary, and so on, and so on." She had a point—and if she weren't so adamant, I probably would have agreed with her. "We cannot have commercials!" she insisted, almost shouting.

"Well, I don't care," I replied, getting a bit adamant myself. "What I've said is said, and I'm not doing it again. If you don't want it, you can edit it out when you get home."

Now she was steaming, because I wouldn't do it again, and I was steaming, because I knew they would take it out, as soon as they got to the editing room. And neither one of us noticed that in the interim, hundreds of villagers had come into the church and had gone into the pews and taken out their rosaries.

All at once, the door to the choir loft opened, and in came Father Slavko with the visionary, Ivan, and a blond woman whom I later learned was the Countess Milona von Hapsburg, who had been converted in Medjugorje and was now Father Slavko's secretary and interpreter.

Down below, the rosary had begun, and I looked to Father Slavko—did he want us to leave?

He shook his head, no, and then he indicated that we should tape Ivan, during the actual apparition. So, because of Barbara's and my squabble, suddenly Heart of the Nation was about to have the extraordinary privilege of taping an apparition.

There was a tiny bench along the outside wall of the choir loft, and I sat on it next to Ivan. Father Slavko and Milona were in one corner, Barbara and the camera crew in the other. We had all joined those below in praying the rosary, when all at once Ivan got up and knelt, facing the west wall of the loft.

Realizing that the apparition was about to occur, I knelt down, too, about eighteen feet behind him. I was watching the camera crew who had the camera on Ivan. Everyone else was staring at the wall, where he was looking.

I did, too, and there was nothing there—at least, nothing that we could see. And now the thoughts tumbled in: You are going to look like a fool! This is going on national television, and you are staring at—nothing! The camera-crew is photographing the wall! And you are propagating something false!

These thoughts began racing through my mind, when immediately there were two flashes of blinding light, as if from a strobe light. Startled, I wondered if someone were using a flash attachment and looked around, but there was no one with a still camera up there, only the video camera.

Then the light flashed again, this time like a streak of lightning, and with it came a mighty wind, of almost hurricane force, it seemed. Immediately I was thrown backwards to the ground from the kneeling position.

On the video, you can hear the wind, and you can also hear two thumps, as first my head and then my feet hit the floor. And you can hear Barbara's voice-over: "This is where Father Roberts hits the ground."

I didn't fall as if shot; it was more like a sledgehammer had hit me! And yet, no one touched me! Only the wind. Afterwards, Barbara told me that I had literally somersaulted backwards—something I could not do from the kneeling position, even as a child.

As I thought about it, I smiled: my first talk that afternoon had been about falling over backwards and trusting God to catch you. I guess occasionally, with some of us, He has to give us a push!

After the apparition was over, and we had come down from the choir loft, people came up: "Did you hear the wind, Father? What *happened* up there?" I didn't want to talk about it; I just wanted to get away and be alone. But Barbara pleaded for a brief interview for the video (which was called "Medjugorje Perspective" and won the Angel Award for Best Religious Documentary of 1988). Could I describe the experience? Not really; it all happened so quickly. What did I feel now? A deep peace—so deep that it was almost euphoric. There was no other way to describe it.

And having said that much, I went to be by myself.

Later, Milona came up to me. "Father Slavko said that something unusual happened today."

"What, me being blown over in the wind?"

"Oh, no," she laughed, "that's happened before."

"Oh," I said, a little disappointed. "What then?"

"Well, every apparition since the beginning has always ended with the Our Father. That's how we know the apparition has ended."

"That didn't happen today?"

"No," she said, bemused, "today it ended with the Magnificat."

And now my third pilgrimage was about to end. On a flight whose departure time had been changed to 3:15. In the corner of the high-ceilinged waiting room, I bowed my head. After the frozen spine and the dark cloud had come and gone, I was not nearly as confident of my imminent demise, as I had been when we started. In fact, after the incident in the choir loft, I felt so spiritually charged, I could hardly wait to get home, to plan my next Medjugorje pilgrimage, and the next. . . .

Still, the prophecy had been specific: my Assembly of God friend had seen the numbers 3:15, and when she heard I was flying overseas, had been quite certain it was a departure time. And now that had come to pass.

Well, if it was just my life, it wouldn't matter. But I had all these young ones which the Lord had entrusted into my care. . . .

There was a gentle tap on my shoulder. It was Annie. Had she changed her mind? Was she coming to me privately, as I had suggested, to ask to go home on a later flight?

"Father Ken, I've been thinking about what you said, and—would you hear my confession?"

"But you just made a confession yesterday, at Medjugorje. You told me it was the most meaningful confession you had ever made—'one to start a new life with,' was what I think you said."

She looked at me, solemn-eyed. "It was. But after what you told us, I remembered a couple of other things that I need to confess. Because if I *am* going to die in an airplane crash, I want my heart to be absolutely clean."

So I motioned for her to take the seat next to me, and I heard the deepest, most penitent confession it had ever been my privilege to hear.

When she finished, she was radiant. "I feel shaky," she

whispered, "but so clean, it's like the Holy Spirit has taken a Brillo pad and scoured me out! Thanks, Father," she added, giving my hand a squeeze.

Thank *you*, Annie, I thought to myself. Inspired by her openness and honesty before her Creator, I asked Him to search the corners of my own heart, for anything that I might have "forgotten," or any place where there might still be unforgiveness. . . .

There was another tap on my shoulder. It was Bill. "Um, Father Ken, I—um," the big but gentle lineman was even more at a loss for words than usual. "Well," he finally blurted out, "would you hear my confession, too?"

"Of course," I smiled, motioning him to take a seat in our makeshift confessional.

A confession, spoken spontaneously from the depths of a contrite soul, is—beautiful; there is no other word for it. The sins being confessed may be as black as soot, yet as they are forgiven and washed away by the Blood of the Lamb, the soul they leave behind is as pure as the driven snow. That afternoon I heard some of the most beautiful confessions in all my years as a priest. As nearly all of them had gone to confession in the last couple of days, they were short. But they were sweet.

And when they were finished, I did my best privately to add my own.

At 2:45, they announced the boarding of our aircraft. As we walked across the tarmac and out to the waiting plane, we had our rosaries in our hands—and peace in our hearts.

6

A Rose Garden

As we climbed the boarding stairs, I noted that the sky
was clearing. There were still heavy storm clouds to the
west, but these were shot through with rays of golden
sunlight. And after all the rain, everything had a fresh-
scrubbed look to it. Even the air seemed to tingle—in all,
more like a beginning than an end.

Entering the cabin, I had to figure out which aisle I
was in and how far back. Instead of greeting us and directing
us to our seats, the stewardesses were having a chat and
a smoke in the galley, oblivious to their passengers. I smiled;
their motto was definitely not: "We take good care of you."

Nor was it just this crew or this airline; the Communist
system seemed to foster an attitude of resentment, or at
best, indifference, in all its service personnel, as anyone
who has ever been at the mercy of a Communist bureaucrat
knows. It extended to schedules: having no competitors,
they did not regard punctuality as a necessary virtue. They
arrived and departed pretty much when they felt like it—

demonstrating, perhaps, that they were not slaves to some other bureaucrat's imposed time-table, or the impatience of foreign travelers.

A movement outside the window caught my eye: the ground crew was rolling back the boarding stairs. Hearing the steward bolt shut the cabin door, I glanced at my watch, and smiled: the one time I would have been just as happy for a further delay, it was precisely 3:15!

As we taxied out to the runway, I recalled from my BOAC training that the most dangerous time on a routine international flight was not the landing (that was second); it was right after take-off, when the plane was carrying a full load of fuel to get it over the ocean. If anything critical happened then—an invisible wind shear or mechanical failure that forced even a minor crash landing—all that fuel would create a holocaust.

In my head, I had settled my account with God and was prepared to rejoin Him, if this was His will and timing. But my heart was still a bit fluttery.

Nothing happened. We were soon smoothly airborne and heading west. And as I often do at the beginning of a long flight, I settled into repose and waited for sleep to come.

It didn't—not completely. I would doze and day-dream and doze again. At one point, I contemplated rousing myself, getting a cup of tea, and putting my mind to some serious praying. Normally my mind was reasonably disciplined. As a student, studying theology or picking up a new language, I discovered that I had an unusual ability for concentration. Now, I would call that a gift— supplemented by a double measure of grace, if what I was learning was something that God had set before me. Chess masters had this ability: they could narrow their focus, until their entire world was confined to 64 squares.

Over the years, I had used this gift, not only to absorb lessons quickly, or in the game of verbal chess known as debating, but as an aid to prayer, in times of uncommon distraction. When I entered the prayer room of my heart, I was able to close the door behind me—and leave it closed, until the Lord indicated that our time together was, for the moment, completed.

But I had already done my serious praying back in the terminal—and now my mind was like an unruly child. Given the possibility that my life might end before I disembarked from this voyage, it seemed bent on reviewing that life, such as it was. But not in episodic, sequential detail; I had already done that, during the writing of *Playboy to Priest*. (If the reader is interested in how one of the most unlikely candidates for the priesthood finally found his calling, it is still in print, published by Our Sunday Visitor.)

No, tonight my mind seemed more like a butterfly in a field of wildflowers, alighting on first one memory then another, never lingering too long, and with no apparent logic to its flight. With a sigh, I relaxed and let it go where it wanted.

It went first to my mother. I could see her kneeling in her garden, pruning, weeding, tying back rose bushes, turning the soil. She spent the most rewarding hours of her life on her knees —- either praying or tending her beloved garden. And it reflected the care she gave it; not even beds in Southampton's main park were as beautiful! Her roses were renowned; their fragrance filled the garden, and people came from miles around, just to see it.

England was famous for her gardens, as anyone who has ever driven through the English countryside could confirm. Because the English were out-of-doors people, they often cared more for their gardens which could be seen, than for the interior of their homes, which could not. Even the poor had gardens—and while I never thought of us as poor when I was growing up, once I started making a great deal of money in the pursuit of happiness, I decided that we were.

In Southampton, as in many English towns, they annually gave a prize to the best garden in the city. My mother had won that prize four years in a row. She would have won it a fifth, but for her eight-year-old son Kenny. The day before the judges came around was Mother's Day, and I wanted to give her something but had no money. I knew she loved flowers. . . .

So I went out to her garden, to the most beautiful flowers in it, the lilies. I pulled them out, cut them off, and went back in the house to present them to her. "Here, Mum, for Mother's Day!"

Tears came to her eyes, as she accepted them.

They were to be the centerpiece of the whole garden that year; she had spent three years cultivating them, and with the rest of the garden they were sure to win the prize. Now there was a gaping hole, where I had pulled them up.

Biting her lip, she gave me a big hug and said, "Mother knows that you love her, and thank you for thinking of me." She took a deep breath, and her voice was quavering but still tender, as she added, "But if you really love me, you won't ever pick the flowers again. Leave them where God has caused them to grow so beautifully. They belong in the garden, not in a vase. Next Mother's Day, just take me out to come look at the flowers with you."

Reliving that moment, and realizing the depth of the pain that my act caused, I could see where I first experienced the forgiving love of Christ through another person. How deep a work He had done in her, for her to respond that way! And what an example of Christ's forgiving love she was for me, then and always!

The butterfly now went to another memory, close by the first. It, too, took place in the garden. I had come home from my first year in seminary for the summer break and was feeling rather sorry for myself. My pride and ego had been dealt with quite severely in a number of areas in that first year of seminary life, as the faculty did their best to prepare me for my vocation. Of course, I didn't see it that way; I thought they were resentful of me for being bright and quick-witted. (I could still bring any class situation to a standstill with my humor—and too often did.)

Looking for my mother, I went out to the garden; always understanding, she would give me the solace I now craved and make me feel special again.

But when I found her, I was shocked: the garden appeared to have been devastated! Her prize rose blooms were strewn all over the walks; there were none left, just bare stalks! This place of tranquility and breathtaking beauty was ugly, with naked thorny stems climbing to the top of the trellis.

Mother stood in the midst of this ruin, surveying her handiwork, wiping her brow with the back of her left hand, while in her right, her trusty Wilkinson pruning shears were poised for any blossom that might have escaped her notice. I was horrified—had she gone mad?

"Mother, why are you doing this?" I asked, after we had hugged.

"Doing what?"

"Destroying all your roses."

"I'm not destroying them, son; I'm pruning them. If I didn't, they'd be wild and would never improve beyond where they are now; in fact, they would gradually diminish. And with these roses, the pruning must be severe—so severe that there won't be very many blooms next year, and there may not even be many the year after. But three years from now, you will see such blooms, as you've never seen in your life!"

I stared at her: it was not the first time the Lord had spoken to me through her, nor would it be the last, but it was certainly the most startling. Needless to say, I said nothing of the pruning I had been experiencing at seminary, and that fall I went back with a different attitude. While I did not exactly appreciate the pruning knife as it was being applied, I reminded myself that I had given the Vinedresser permission—and then prayed for the grace to accept it.

I smiled now at that recollection: had I had any inkling of how much pruning would be required. . .

There was a tap on my shoulder. I looked up at the non-smiling stewardess. "Dinner?" she inquired. When I shook my head, she shrugged and moved on to the next row.

And I went back to the field, to see where the butterfly would go next.

7

The Hound of Heaven

Settling back into my seat, I gazed dreamily out the window. There was a solid overcast below, but up here we were enjoying a spectacular sunset—and a long one, for we were flying west with the sun. But the sun was outdistancing us, leaving behind a sky that was shading imperceptibly from scarlet to crimson to purple and night.

Behind me, the cabin was darkened. The movie projector didn't work, and one by one the reading lights went out, as passengers tried to get some sleep. I dozed again, then lingered in that state just below wakefulness. The butterfly had alighted on another memory, of the Via Veneto, in Rome.

Back in my BOAC days, of all our destinations, Rome was my favorite. It was the penultimate party town, and we always brought dinner jackets and gowns when we were going to Rome. In those days there was not a more glamorous avenue in the world than the Via Veneto, with its fabulous restaurants and all the famous cafes with their

49

white tables in front. . . . We would start at the top, at Harry's American, and work our way down. And late in the evening, we might drop by L'Osteria Del Orso, to listen to Enzo Samaritini sing ballads.

One evening, before such an outing, I was having a capuccino in the hotel's coffee shop, when I recognized another BOAC chief steward. Bob was in black tie, and I asked him where he was going. "To the best club on the Via Veneto," he replied.

"Really? Which one?"

"Madame Bricktop's."

"Never heard of it—and I thought I knew them all."

"Well, you'd better join me, then," and I did.

In the cab on the way over, he filled me in on the owner. Before the war, she had run an establishment for "ladies of questionable virtue" in Paris. She was a favorite of cafe society there—so much so, that she was the inspiration for Cole Porter's infamous ballad, "Miss Otis Regrets."

After the war, she opened up a very high-class club on the Via Veneto, where ladies could be picked up. But now there was a difference: during the war, one of her former workers had been converted and was now a priest, studying in Rome. This had intrigued her: what could cause a man like that to become converted? What intrigued her even more was how the Church could accept someone of his background.

Out of curiosity she arranged to meet him, and when he introduced her to Fr. Cunningham, pastor of Santa Suzanna, the American church in Rome, she could not resist describing her occupation in the most lurid terms.

"Are you trying to shock me?" asked Fr. Cunningham with a smile, and now it was she who was taken aback.

"Because if you heard half of what I hear every day in the confessional, *you* would be the one who was shocked!"

Thus began an interesting and ongoing relationship, which resulted in her taking instruction to become a Catholic. Nor did she stop there; she put her money where her heart was, subtly changing her club to make it a channel for God's work. She was still the darling of the jet-set, and she would still sing the old songs for them, but now there was something different. . . .

By this time, I had mixed emotions about what lay in store for us this evening. As fascinated as I was at the prospect of meeting the former madam, Madame Bricktop, I had the funny feeling that somehow the hound of heaven was on my track again. . . .

Her night club had a '30's look to it, all Art Deco and mirrors, darkly lit, indirect lighting—as posh as anyone could ask for. We were early enough to get seats, and I did not realize at first that our hostess was also the floor show's featured attraction. She sang in the style of Sophie Tucker, and as she came to the last song of her set, she drew out a crucifix and said, "And now I want to dedicate this song to my boyfriend, Jesus Christ," and she kissed the crucifix. I was startled—but the way she did it, it was not offensive.

Afterwards, she came around to the different tables, asking people if they would like to contribute to the local orphanage she was helping to support. "Getting milk out of whiskey glasses," she called it, when she stopped to chat with us.

As we talked, before I knew what was happening, I was telling her my life's story. And when I had finished, she looked at me, her head tilted, and said: "You know, I think God is still calling you to be a priest."

Impossible, I explained: I was engaged, and besides I was enjoying life far too much, to give it up for the priesthood. But she would not be dissuaded; in fact, she told me that she would pray for me. And then she said: "Tell you what, there's a little shrine outside the gates, right opposite Tre Fontani, where St. Paul was beheaded. A Communist who had been attempting to assassinate Pius XII was hiding in a cave there, with his two children, when the Blessed Virgin Mary appeared to them. It changed his life."

I looked at her, as if she was crazy. "It's an approved site," she hastened to add, misinterpreting my expression, but I just shook my head; I could not believe the whole thing!

"Here," she declared, putting a piece of paper in front of me. "You write the Blessed Mother a note, and I'll take it out there for you, Sunday."

"What?" I exclaimed. "Write who? What are you talking about?" The woman was obviously a few cards short of a full deck! Still, she had a good heart, and so I decided to humor her. Taking out a pen, I said, "Um, I've never written the, uh —"

"The Blessed Mother. Just write something like: 'Blessed Mother, please show me what you want me to do.' "

This was so strange—I looked around at all the well-dressed people in their dinner jackets and gowns, laughing, drinking, having a good time. . . . and in this setting I was about to write a message to the Mother of God! I would do well to check my own deck of cards!

Then I glanced at our hostess; she was waiting, her eyes pleading. Oh, well, I sighed, in for a penny, in for a pound. . . .

I took the piece of paper and wrote: *Blessed Mother, please show me what you want me to do,* and handed it to her.

With a beautiful smile, she thanked me, folded it up, tucked it away, and left.

As did we.

So now, in addition to my mother, I had this extraordinary woman from the Via Veneto praying for me.

There was some minor turbulence, and then we were flying smoothly again. Looking down, I saw that we had sailed over the edge of the overcast; now, thousands of feet below, the surface of the ocean glistened in the moonlight like a wet, black slate.

I closed my eyes and returned to the field, to see where the butterfly would go next.

When I saw where it next alighted, my nose wrinkled: the streets of Calcutta. I never cared for that city when I was with BOAC; too many beggars, too many abandoned, huddled wretches too weak to brush the flies from their faces, too many sacred cows dropping sacred dung on the sidewalks. . . As much as I loved Rome, I loathed Calcutta.

On the occasion I was remembering, I was on a special mission: some very well-to-do friends of my mother's had asked me to do them a great favor: their daughter had become converted. In many families, that would be cause for rejoicing, but not in this one.

When their daughter started attending Mass every day, they thought it was just a phase that she would pass through. But when she lost interest in young men (and this was a very attractive, very popular young lady), and began speaking of going to Calcutta to work with Mother Teresa, their concern grew into alarm.

And then one day, she simply left. The next thing they knew, they received a letter—from Calcutta. She had been accepted into the novitiate of Mother Teresa's order and was now helping those from whom everyone else had turned away. She assured them that she had never been happier in her life.

Her parents had never been more miserable. Someone needed to go out there and bring her to her senses! Her father was willing—but she would never listen to him. No, it should be someone she knew—what about young Roberts? He was a persuasive fellow, and he was certainly doing well at BOAC. If anyone could remind her of all that the world had to offer her, he could.

So, off I went on this knight's errand, to rescue a damsel in distress. As usual, I packed my dinner jacket—but the Calcutta of Mother Teresa was far different from the one I was accustomed to. When BOAC stopped there, I would dine atop the finest hotel, surrounded by gleaming silver and crystal and crisp white linen—far above the hunger and despair in the teeming streets below.

Now, as I found my way to their convent, my custom-made shoes were soon fouled, and the stench was enough to make one's eyes water. When I arrived, the new sister invited me into their parlor and offered me tea.

While she poured, I simply stared at her. . . She wore no make-up, her features were hardly glamorous, her blue-edged white habit could not have been more plain. Yet she was the most beautiful woman I had ever seen. I was speechless.

She passed me a cup and waited, a half-smile at the corner of her lips. When I did not say anything, she spoke: "So—what brings you to our convent?"

I sensed she already knew—or at least suspected. We

made small talk, and then I did my best. "You know how much your mother and father love you. They've devoted their lives to you, and they can't understand why you've done this. It makes no rational sense to them whatever— or to me, I must confess."

I paused to give her opportunity to reply, but she just looked at me. There was about her, a quiet radiance that was almost ethereal. And in her steady grey eyes was an inner beauty. . . . the eyes have been called the window to the soul; looking in hers, I saw more than happiness— I saw serenity.

Realizing that I was staring again, I tried to re-focus on my mission: "Your parents—all that they have always enjoyed, they had hoped to pass on to you, and now—"

"Kenneth, why have you come?"

Disconcerted, I blurted out, "I mean, how can you be so happy, living in such filth?" There was an edge in my voice now—and not for her parents, for myself. Because in walking away from everything that they had invested their lives in, she had done the same to everything *I* valued.

She smiled and asked me the same question: "How can *you* be happy, living in such filth?"

"But I'm living in luxury!"

"You are living solely for yourself. In the eyes of God," she paused, and her glance seemed to take in the tailored silk, the Egyptian cotton, the patent leather, "that is filth. Insidious filth, eating away at your soul."

I was speechless—this time with anger! How dare she—

"Kenneth, God wants you to live selflessly—for Him, not for you." Those steady grey eyes would not release mine. "And you know it."

"I know no such thing!" I exclaimed, "and what's more, I—"

She got up. "From now on, I am going to pray every day for you. I am going to pray that you accept your call."

"What call?" I almost shouted.

"You are called to become a priest," she smiled, extending her hand. "I will pray that you do."

"Well," I said with sarcasm, but returning her smile, as we shook hands good-bye, "you'd better believe in miracles then."

"Oh, but I do!" she beamed.

And so then there were three handmaidens of the Lord, praying for my conversion—my mother, a certain Madame in Rome, and a grey-eyed nun in Calcutta.

The hound was growing closer by the day.

8

By the Sea

Somewhere in the night I awoke and took a stroll around the darkened cabin to stretch my limbs. Everyone else was asleep, even the steward and stewardesses. Resuming my seat, I settled back down, and gazed out the window.

Outside, the night was breathtakingly clear, and the stars shone with an icy brilliance. We were approaching another front—which had piled clouds before it like a range of mountains, reaching almost as high as we were. In the ghostly light of the half-moon, their outcroppings gleamed like snow-shrouded granite.

Glancing at my watch, I realized I must have slept longer than I thought; there were only four hours left. With a yawn, I settled back down—but my mind was not ready for more sleep. The butterfly, it seemed, had one more summer flower to investigate. . . .

Beirut. It was hard to believe now, but that tragic shambles was once called "the Paris of the Mediterranean." Cosmopolitan and sophisticated, in 1959 it catered to international dilettantes who were bored with Nice and Cannes, and looking for something different. Last year it was Dubrovnik, this year Beirut, next year. . . .

On the evening in question, our crew had a three-day layover in Beirut and had just checked in at the Bristol, on a hill not far from the harbor, where we always stayed. And since there was another BOAC crew there already, and someone had called a friend on the PanAm flight which had just arrived, we had the makings of a first-class party.

We reserved the hotel's largest suite. What we normally did was congregate there in the early afternoon, as soon as everyone could get changed, and drink there until it was time to go out to dinner. The party would go en masse to the best restaurant, and then start clubbing. We would go from place to place till everything closed, and repair back to the party suite, to carry on until dawn. Then we would have two days to recover.

That afternoon, as it happened, someone's plane or yacht had also arrived, disgorging a load of rich vagabonds who were asking where the action was. Since that was wherever BOAC was, our party was shaping up to be a classic.

The only problem was, I had not slept in two days. Normally, I could just shake it off; a few glasses of the bubbly, and I would be good till at least three o'clock in the morning. But this afternoon I was dead on my feet. So I told my friends to go on without me; I would take a quick nap, and catch up before they knew I was among the missing.

Only I was more tired than I thought; three full hours passed, before I finally woke up. I dressed hurriedly, not wanting them to go off to dinner without me. The party suite was on the second floor, with a balcony overlooking the Mediterranean. Still half asleep, I got there a little after six and was relieved to find that the party hadn't moved on without me. On the contrary, it was in full swing.

If partying is your way of life, the one thing you don't ever want to do is show up at one sober, when your friends are three sheets to the wind. Because you will see them in a different light. And then you will be faced with a difficult choice: either you must quickly down a couple of drinks to catch up, or. . . .

Someone passed me glass of champagne, but I smiled and waved my hand. "In a minute," I murmured. "I've only just woken up."

I stood at the end of the bar, surveying what was going on—and I was stunned. After three hours of partying on nothing to eat, everyone was raucous and crude and laughing inanely and pawing one another. There was an underlying frantic urgency to the scene, as if they were trying desperately hard to have fun—and not quite succeeding. Here and there, couples were doing things that most people would not do even in private; in all, it was—well, if someone were staging a scene of utter depravity, they could not have done better.

I was nauseated—in soul and spirit, as well as body. *This* was the jet-set? These people were animals! More like beasts than humans—and I wondered if this was how Dante imagined the first circle of the Inferno.

A giggling young-old woman, half out of her dress, came up to me with a bottle of Dom Perignon and managed to spill some on me, before I could say no. Revulsed, I started towards the door. Then another woman, very elegant, and very definitely not from a flight crew, was suddenly sick all over herself and her companion. As the

vomit dripped from her designer dress, I clapped a hand
to my own mouth and got out of there.

Having grown up in a seaport, in later life, whenever
I wanted to do some thinking, I got by the water. If it
couldn't be the ocean, then a river or a lake or even a
swimming pool would do. That evening, the sun was about
to set on the Mediterranean, as I took a cab down to the
shore. It was the dinner hour, and so I had the beautiful
beach of Beirut almost to myself.

I picked a large boulder and sat down to watch the
gentle waves advance and recede. There was a rhythm to
them—and I found myself saying the rosary to their
accompaniment. The phrases fit the ebb and flow
perfectly—as if the sea and I were praying them together.

I thought of my mother, praying this prayer for years
before I was born—and all the years she had prayed for
me since then, without ever giving up. I thought of the sister
in Calcutta, who had walked away from the life I had chosen,
and who had put the same question to me, that I had put
to her: "How can you live in such filth?" I had thought
then that she was crazy; I had a new penthouse flat in
London, a sporty Rover, a growing bank account. . . .

If someone had asked me then: what was the purpose
of life? I would have told them: have as much fun as you
can, as long as you don't hurt anyone in the process.

But after what I had just come from, I was not at all
sure—in fact, I was no longer certain of anything. Nothing
I had ever witnessed in my life had shaken me as that
party had. If that was the best that my life had to offer,
then I was embracing hell.

"Blessed Mother!" I groaned aloud, "Please help me!" I could not remember praying to her like that before, but I felt close to her nonetheless, probably because of my own mother. And she was the one I prayed to, because I was so ashamed of who I was, and what I was becoming, that I could not bear to come before a heavenly Father. But a mother—could forgive anything.

The little waves plashed ashore and withdrew, and gradually I felt calmer. For some reason, the catechism I had learned as a child, now came back to me. It provided a slightly different perspective on the purpose of life: "God made me to know Him, to love Him, and to serve Him."

I stared out at the fiery copper disc of the sun, now sinking into the Mediterranean Sea. Just before it disappeared, its last ray drew a line to the shore where I was sitting.

Dusk was gathering; stretching, I got to my feet and thought about taking a cab back to the hotel. But I was in no hurry to go back there—and so I walked along the sidewalk next to the beach. Soon it was night, but it was still warm, and doors were left open for the breeze. Through the door of a church, I heard singing that sounded familiar, from a long time ago. It was Latin—and as I stopped and listened, I recognized the Gregorian Chant that went with the Benediction service.

I had not been to Benediction since I was a child. Back then, it was something done in the evening, as Mass was for the mornings. Suddenly it seemed to have a tremendous appeal—I turned and mounted the steps.

Inside, it seemed like many a Catholic church—there was a statue of Mary, the votive candles, the Stations of the Cross on the wall. . . . But the congregation was dressed entirely in long, white robes. In fact, they reminded me of the paintings of Mary and Joseph; it was as if I had been transported back in time some two thousand years! They could not have been more alien in their garb or appearance, yet they were worshipping exactly as I had, as millions had all over the world. *Yesterday, today, and forever.* . . .

Normally, even at home I would have been self-conscious, being the only man in church in black tie and dinner jacket. And here, I was the only Westerner in a congregation of Lebanese. *A stranger, in a strange land.* . . . and all I felt was peace.

In my head, I always thought I knew the meaning of the word "catholic," but now in my heart the Holy Spirit was showing me the depth and breadth of its true meaning. It was the Church universal, in all corners of the world, in all ages of history. *As it was, and is, and ever shall be.* . . .

It was the Body of Christ on earth—comprised of all who worshipped at the foot of His Cross, regardless of nationality or liturgical form. If you loved Him—if you knew that He had given His life for you, that you might be redeemed and belong to Him for eternity, if, in the meantime, you wanted Him to rule and reign in your heart—then you were part of His Body.

I was part of that Body—as much as the dark-skinned, white-robed man kneeling beside me. As much as all the men and women who had knelt in this place in all the years before now—and all the years to come. We were one.

The Blessed Sacrament was on the altar. It was in a gold monstrance, which resembled a clock on a stand, with rays emanating from the extra-large circular host, visible behind glass at its center. As soon as I was old enough to understand, my mother had explained to me that this was indeed the Body of Christ—His Body, which had been broken for me.

And now the priest, with his humeral veil over his shoulders and hands (for it would not be he that would give the blessing to the people; that would come from Christ Himself, present in the Eucharist), elevated the host above his head, preparing to make the sign of the Cross.

Looking up at the Blessed Sacrament, I felt shame—but also hope, for He had come, not for the righteous, but for sinners. Like me. There were tears in my eyes, then; I couldn't pray, couldn't find the words. But He could see my heart.

As the priest brought the monstrance down, the altar boy rang the bell—just as I had, many years ago. Suddenly I felt pins and needles all over. Then came this warmth—it was as if I was bathed in invisible sunlight, from the top of my head down to my toes, and from the inside, out.

God was pouring out His Spirit upon me, as Joel had prophesied He would, before the Day of the Lord. I felt tingly all over—and so joyful that I took care not to laugh out loud, lest I disrupt the service. Something did come out, however—words that I had never heard before. I, the linguist, was speaking a language that I could not identify. Nor did I have any knowledge of the meaning of the words I was speaking—at least, not with my head.

I think my heart understood perfectly: we were praising God and thanking Him for forgiving me, and for His love, and His wonderful mercy.

Love was the operative word. I felt overwhelming love for everyone in that church—everyone everywhere, in fact. God *was* love, and His Spirit was indwelling me, and—

A few of the people in long robes glanced at me—I don't know if they understood what I was saying, but from my expression they certainly understood what I was feeling! And they smiled back.

I felt happily disconnected. My head was jealous of what my heart and I were experiencing. It did not understand what was taking place (this being many years prior to the Charismatic Renewal in the Catholic Church); as far as it was concerned, I was speaking gibberish. And now, to make matters worse, there were tears coming! Not tears of sorrow or grief, they were tears of cleansing—"the window-washing of the soul," someone called them.

Next, the thought came: *Go to confession.* I looked around for a confessional, and there was one, with a priest in it. He couldn't speak English, and I couldn't speak Arabic, so we made do in French.

That night did not mark the end of my pursuit of the rich life. It did, however, mark the beginning of the end.

"The captain has lit the seat belt sign," the steward informed us with a yawn. "We will be landing in New York in a few minutes." Well, I thought, if there was anything to that prophecy, it was about to happen. If this was it, I was as ready as I would ever be. *Come, Lord Jesus, come.*

And sure enough, just as our plane was committed to its final approach and reaching down for the runway with its landing gear, a crosswind picked up. The pilot had to yaw to the left and then back again, to re-align with the runway. As it was, we lurched a little on touch-down, and the tires chirped a bit. But then we were rolling out—and behind me, our young people gave a great cheer.

The plane nestled up to the passenger gangway that came out to us, and we collected our carry-on luggage from the overhead compartments. As we walked the long corridor to where we would collect our baggage prior to clearing customs, Annie took my arm. She was smiling *and* frowning. "Father Ken," she murmured, looking around to make sure no one was in earshot, "this is weird: I think I'm a little disappointed that something *didn't* happen. I mean, I was so *ready!*"

I chuckled and nodded; I knew exactly what she meant.

I thought the story was over, but it wasn't. There was a final, intriguing postscript, one that put all the pieces in place. But it would have to wait until I got back home to St. Louis.

9

Genesis 3:15

In St. Louis, I was the extraordinary confessor to the Carmelite Sisters, a cloistered order whose confessions I heard four times a year. After hearing them, we would visit, and I would give them a "pep talk," encouraging them on their demanding walk. Usually they wound up encouraging me as much as I did them, and my next meeting with them was no exception.

They always wanted to know where I'd been and what I was doing, and so, not surprisingly, the subject of my talk that day was prophetic warnings—and how to regard them. On the one hand, you treated them with respect, because they might indeed be from God. But you kept in mind that they were coming through human filters which might be far from perfect.

If they were alarming in nature, you should be concerned but not fearful—for they might not be from God. The enemy was adept at imitating divine prophecy, and often very convincing. If you were at all in doubt, you should pray for a double measure of discernment and submit the warning to the judgment of a trusted friend or spiritual director. Eventually the enemy would give himself away: either the prophetic word would become directive or accusative, or its tone would become strident or harsh.

If the prophecy *was* a warning from God, then He would confirm it in other ways. The main thing was to make certain that you were moving in His will and timing for you; if you were, then He would take care of the rest. And by way of illustration, I outlined the warnings I had received prior to my recent trip.

"So you see," I concluded, "the best-intentioned prophecy still comes through fallible human instruments and is not always correct. You weigh it, you invite the evaluation of a spiritual director or a friend in whose discernment you have confidence. But above all, you double-check your own guidance: *Is* God calling you? Then go. *Not* to go would be disobedient. In fact, in my case these prophecies that never came to pass may have been a maneuver of Satan to keep me from going."

I chuckled. "And just look what would have happened, had I stayed home—or rather, what would *not* have happened: I would not have been involved in 20/20's documentary, and Heart of the Nation would not have gone—and filmed that incredible footage with the wind and the lights and the sound of Father Roberts' backward somersault!"

They all laughed—all, save one old nun who was shaking her head. "You don't agree?" I asked her.

"But they *did* come true," she insisted in a frail voice, and I realized that she must be close to ninety.

"What do you mean, sister?"

"Well, the frozen spine: did you get that in Medjugorje?"

I nodded. "As a matter of fact, I did."

"And the black cloud—you said it was there in the Heart of the Nation film."

"That's true. But here I am, sitting here, talking with you all: *I didn't crash.*"

"Yes, you did."

"I did?"

"Father, you crashed in the balcony—what else would you call it?"

"Hmm—well, what about the plane at 3:15?"

Now the old nun smiled. "She was a Protestant," she announced, as if that explained everything.

"Who was?"

"Your friend in Omaha—you said that she was Assembly of God."

"But, sister, what does that have to do with it?"

"Everything! You crashed in front of the Blessed Mother, just as she was appearing."

"And?"

"A Protestant might not regard Genesis 3:15 with the same significance that we do."

A light finally went on: we took that particular verse— *I shall put enmity between you and the woman, and between your offspring and hers*—as referring not only to the future relationship between Eve (and all women) and the serpent, but specifically to the spiritual battle which would take place between the Blessed Mother and Satan. For us, this was the first reference to Mary in the Bible.

I was stunned; it should have occurred to me, as that verse was where I often began, when talking about Mary. "You know, sister," I said slowly, "you're right. And now that I think of it, all she *got* was '3:15' and the word 'Crash.' Putting the two together and knowing I was a frequent

flier, she had *assumed* it referred to an airplane—as anyone
might have. But there was actually nothing about an
airplane in the prophecy that she had been given for me!"

Genesis 3:15 was a favorite verse of mine, whenever
I discussed the doctrinal differences between Catholics and
Protestants. For it was the Catholics' regard for Mary that
was invariably the greatest stumbling block they had to
our becoming one in spirit—what I considered to be true
ecumenism.

Not long after my return from Medjugorje in that summer
of '88, I had an encouraging ecumenical experience, in
which Mary, instead of being a barrier, was the bridge.
A bishop in Central America invited me to come down
to his tiny country to preach a week-long mission in the
cathedral. At that time throughout Latin America, Protestant
Evangelical and Charismatic churches, with their sound
Biblical teaching and enthusiastic belief that God still
answered prayer, often with miracles, were drawing millions
of Catholics away from their traditional faith.

The situation was critical. They had one television
channel, on which was featured a certain televangelist who
was rabidly anti-Catholic. As an antidote, the local Jesuits
were broadcasting "Catholic Beliefs and Practices," a series
I did to remind Catholics that their own doctrine was equally
well-grounded in Scripture, and that God would do miracles
for us, too, if we asked Him, believing. So the Jesuits went
to the bishop and suggested, "Let's get this guy Roberts
down here to preach a mission."

Let me say at the outset: I have no objection to Protestants
remaining Protestant. I am not trying to win them to

Catholicism (if God wants to do that, that's His business). I just wish they would be content to let us remain Catholic. Because I do believe that if God has placed an infant in a Catholic family, then He has a plan for him or her in that context. Which is why, if I meet someone who has left Catholicism, because it seems to offer less than some other denomination, I feel no compunction about showing them just how much the Catholic faith *does* have to offer.

One thing I do envy about Protestantism is its strong emphasis on familiarity with the Bible. Too many Catholics are just not aware of what is in the Word of God. If you have never read the Bible all the way through, you should. Start with the Gospels (and read them as the inspired Word of God, not literature), then read the rest of the New Testament, and all of the Old. *Don't* skip, *do* read a reasonable amount every day, and it will take you about a year.

As for which denomination (or sect or chapter or church) is *right*—that question, with its powerful appeal to self-righteousness and spiritual pride, is the main tool with which the enemy has so effectively divided and neutralized the Body of Christ for so long.

If you can accept the tenets of the Nicean Creed, if you can affirm that Jesus is Lord, then I am your brother. And as you and I kneel at the foot of His Cross, gazing up with eyes only for Him, then we are one.

We must be careful, however, not to give the impression that all religions are the same. All religions have some truth, and we should be searching to find the greatest amount of that truth.

When I arrived, I discovered that a great deal of effort had gone into preparing for and publicizing my mission. There were banners and posters, and the first night, the cathedral was packed to overflowing; in fact, judging from the gigantic crowd in the street for which they had put up loudspeakers, there may have been more people outside than inside.

It was warm in the cathedral; most of the men were in short-sleeved white shirts, and the women in white cotton dresses. And there was a sense of anticipation; the air almost crackled with it.

I was sitting next to the bishop who was presiding, and before we began, he leaned over and murmured: "The Assembly of God minister is here this evening."

"Where?"

"In the last pew, just to the left of the door—the man in the seersucker suit." He told me of his background: originally a Catholic, he had been evangelized by the American televangelist who had been there. Now ordained as an Assembly of God minister, he, more than anyone else, had been responsible for proselytizing Catholics out of the Church. Indeed, his own church was the fastest growing congregation in the city. And tonight he was here, to listen to my mission.

That night I preached on God the Father—a straight-forward message I had given often before, though each time the Holy Spirit seemed to add something, so that it sounded fresh, even to my ears. The second night, I preached on God the Son, also basic, Trinitarian material. The Evangelical minister had come back, only now he was sitting in the middle of the congregation.

The third night, I preached on the Church, and the Mystical Body of Christ, and for this he was in the front row.

The week went quickly, and each night there seemed to be even more people than before. When the last evening's talk was over, the bishop stepped to the microphone. "I have some news for you: we have had a miracle here this evening! The Pentecostal minister, whom all of you know, has been reconciled to the Church. He has been to Confession, and he has come home!"

There was pandemonium, as the people went crazy! They were cheering the re-conversion, yes—but they were also rejoicing at the end to the unholy, holy war that had caused such dissension in their city.

While everyone was celebrating, I kept hoping that he was still there; I wanted to talk to him privately. He was, and I did. In a vacant office I said, "I knew you were here, but I didn't know why."

"I'd come to see what you would say, so that if there was anything I didn't agree with, I could expose your faulty doctrine in *my* service. And believe me, I had my Bible and notebook handy. But to everything you said about God the Father, all I could say was Amen!"

He smiled, a little embarrassed. "So I came back the second night, and you talked about Jesus the Lord, the second Person of the Trinity, the Lord and Saviour, the Alpha, the Omega, Jesus Christ truly God, Jesus Christ truly Man, Jesus, the Son of Mary—and once again, all I could do was agree with you, totally!"

He smiled at the recollection. "Well, the next night you were going to talk about the Mystical Body, and that night I sat down in front—so close I could hear your accent, because now I was going to nail you!"

He laughed. "But everything you said made perfect sense! There was not one thing which I did not believe, also. I even told the person next to me: 'We're on the same track; I believe what he believes.' "

I waited, intrigued, but finally I had to ask: "What was it that brought you back to the Church?"

"Your talk on Mary."

I stared at him. "I would have thought that would be the one thing which would have turned you off. What was it I said about Mary that convinced you?"

He hesitated, then said, "It was when you asked the question: 'How can you have a second Adam, without a second Eve?' " He shook his head. "You know it's true: we Pentecostals believe that Christ is the second Adam. It's in Romans."

I nodded. "Just as through the first Adam, all have died, so through the new Adam, Christ, all are saved."

"So," he went on, "when you asked: 'Where is your second Eve?' I realized that I had no answer; Pentecostalism had no answer. And, well—here I am."

I embraced him and welcomed him.

The ironic thing was, I had not said all that I usually did about Mary; I had not gone into Genesis 3:15, and the Church's teaching on the Immaculate Conception.

This verse which had been so significant on my third pilgrimage to Medjugorje, was to become part of every pilgrimage I would lead there (as of this writing, there have been twenty). Because for anyone going to Medjugorje, Mary was obviously the place to begin.

I soon found that Protestants were not the only ones who had problems with Mary; there were many Catholics, even priests, who shared the Protestants' misconceptions and thus did not have any devotion to her at all, let alone the right one.

Conversely, there were many who loved her but had a wrong understanding of her. In their extreme devotion, they cast her in a role which was not her rightful place— and because it was a false devotion, it turned many others away from her entirely.

One extreme is as out of balance as the other, and both have done a great deal of harm—which is why I feel it so important to make the point that Mary is the second Eve.

To begin at the beginning: Protestants and Catholics have no problem with the fact that God created Adam in His own image. Look at the story in Genesis: He created man in His own image, and He was finished. *Then* He felt sorry for the man—and from him he took a woman. If you read the Scripture carefully, you see that her creation was almost like an afterthought. It was not that God needed a woman; He was perfect, complete. But He felt sorry for the man; it was the *man* who needed the woman.

What happened then? Adam, whose name means "man," called her Eve, which means "mother of the living," and now Eve disobeys God. Her "no" caused Adam to say "no", and we have the Fall. This was the original sin, and ever since, according to my Protestant friends, we have awaited another man, a second Adam, to get us out of it.

But where is the balance in that for a woman? Are we to blame the woman for getting us into the mess, and absolve the man? And now we have to wait for another man to save us and get us out of our troubles? It sounds a bit chauvinistic, even to me. It is not the Catholic position.

Theologically, the Catholic position would be that God created man and woman, equally—"male and female He made them." True, He did make the man first—but you know, if you try a key in a lock, and it doesn't fit, what do you do? You try it the other way around.

In a way, that's what God did. Not that the first way was wrong; He just reversed the process in the *new* creation. In the first, He made the man first, and from the man He took the woman. In the new creation, He makes the new Eve first, and from her He takes the new Adam. The lock is unlocked.

But where, ask my Protestant friends, is that in Scripture? Once at an ecumenical gathering, with many ministers from many denominations, we were sharing our faith, and when we got onto Mary, the division came. One of them said: "Where can you Catholics defend the Immaculate Conception, from the Bible?"

So I asked all the Bible preachers there—the Baptist and the Lutheran and the Presbyterian and the Disciples of Christ and the Methodist and so on—to open their Bibles to Genesis 3:15. I asked them, "What does that mean to you? Who is this seed of hers, who's going to crush the serpent's head?"

"Well, that's Christ," they declared. "Don't you believe that?"

"Of course I do," I replied. I glanced at them, one by one. "Does everyone agree that this is a prophetic reference to Christ, who will crush the serpent's head?" They all nodded. In the King James version, it said, "it shall bruise thy head;" in the Douay version, it said "she;" in the New Ecumenical Bible it said, "they." I was not worried about the seed.

I said, "If we all agree on the second half of Genesis 3:15, what about the first half? Do you ever preach on half a verse? Do you ever get up, open the Bible, and say, 'This morning we're going to look at John, chapter six, verse one and a half?' "

They laughed, and I said, "So, we've got to look at the whole of Genesis 3:15, and the first half is a prophetic reference to the woman: 'I will put enmity between you, Satan, and the woman, between your seed and her seed.' Enmity means complete separation. Which means she can *never* be under the dominion of Satan—not even in her conception. If at any moment in her existence, she were under the devil, the separation would not be complete; there would not be enmity." I looked around; some were beginning to see where I was going.

"The problem, I think, is with people's idea of conception. When you speak of the Immaculate Conception, many people, Catholics included, think it means the *way* that Mary was conceived, the conceptual act. But it has nothing to do with that."

Now there were a few furrowed brows. "Look," I explained, "think of a cathedral or a great painting, or the Pietà. The Pietà is Michelangelo's conception. St Peter's in Rome is an architect's conception; Notre-Dame in Paris is another. But when man conceives of something, it begins in his mind, then he makes a sketch, then he or someone draws up a plan, and then he or someone builds it. There's a sequence."

Heads nodded—they were with me again. "But with God, it's different: when God conceives, it is. When He says: "Let there be light," there's light. God conceived light, it existed. God conceived life, it existed. When God conceived Adam, did He conceive him without sin? Yes. When God conceived Eve, did He conceive her without sin? Yes. Adam and Eve were immaculately conceived— and that's what the Church means by that."

It grew still. "And Mary, the second Eve, the Church is saying, was also conceived by God without sin—through God Himself, through the anticipated merits of Christ, her Son."

"But," the Presbyterian minister asked, "doesn't she say in," he checked his Bible, "Luke 1:46 (RSV), 'My soul magnifies the Lord, and my spirit rejoices in God my Saviour'—did He save her?"

"Of course He saved her."

"But if she was 'without sin,' what did He save her *from*?"

"From sin, anticipated." I paused, realizing I needed to explain. "If you were drowning, and someone dragged you out of the sea and gave you resuscitation, that person would be your saviour. If that same person kept you from entering the water, he would still be your saviour, even though you weren't drowning."

"I can see that," he said, nodding.

"Mary received *before* birth, what we receive after. God, anticipating her perfect obedience—her "yes," even to her Son going to the Cross—preserved her from original sin. As this was also in anticipation of the merits of her Son, He is her Saviour, saving her, even before conception, from any stain of sin."

I looked at them. "In the mind of God, we inherit Adam's fallen nature. When we are re-born in Christ, we are restored to an immaculate condition, washed clean by the blood He shed for us at Calvary, and freed forever from the bondage of sin. That was what St. Paul was referring to, in his second letter to the Corinthians, when he spoke of the old passing away, and all being new (5:17). Now we are a new creation, a new conception. We may still sin—we still have free will—but now there is available to us the means of being forgiven again, cleansed again, renewed again."

They all nodded; they'd preached the same thing, countless times. "But Mary didn't need to be renewed. She was already conceived without sin at her conception by the power of God, anticipating the merits of Christ, her Son. That's why she is the new Eve—from whom the new Adam is taken." Q.E.D.

Thinking about that, it seems to me that what is really important is the balance: Christ is truly God and truly Man. He is the second person of the Trinity, and therefore, Lord of Lords and King of Kings, equal with the Father and the Spirit, and as such, only He can receive adoration and glory.

But it was not as God that He saved us; it was as Man. We inherited sin through Adam, and it was as Adam that Christ saved us; He took his place. As Paul put it in his first letter to the believers at Corinth: "For as in Adam all die; in Christ, shall all be made alive" (15:22). He confirmed that, in his letter to the Romans, where he refers to the first Adam as a prefiguring of Him who is to come (5:14).

So, we have all gained new life through the new Adam. Just as the original Adam and Eve said "no" to God in the Garden at the tree of disobedience, so Jesus and Mary, the new Adam and the new Eve, both say "yes" at the tree of obedience, the Cross. That is the Church's teaching on the Immaculate Conception. Mary's role now is not as a goddess, but as a second Eve—a "mother of the living."

Before ending the chapter on Genesis 3:15, there's one more story about the Immaculate Conception: it happened to me almost exactly a year ago—at a black, very poor inner-city church in the Philadelphia area. Because of its location, I did not expect a large turn-out—and I could not have been more wrong! The church was big and beautiful, and it was packed out, like St. James in Medjugorje—standing room only, with precious little of that!

When I got there, I discovered that it was not going to be a Mass, as I had anticipated; it was going to be a rosary and sermon and Benediction. I had been told that, of course, but had forgotten. (Speaking two, three, and even four times a day, I find myself forgetting too often—and even more, with each passing year.) It was not a problem in a Mass; I usually preached on the Scripture readings assigned for that day. But tonight, there was not going to be a Mass; it was up to me what I preached on.

Surveying the scene, I noted the Blessed Sacrament on the altar—that was it: I would preach on the Eucharist.

I did not ask God, if He *wanted* me to preach on the Eucharist; I did not seek His guidance at all. I decided what we would preach on, and expected Him to approve my decision—and anoint it.

From a priest, I borrowed a Bible, and in it I put markers at all the passages I would need, to give the whole background of the Eucharist from the Old Testament, and then link it up with the New. They were going to receive one comprehensive theological dissertation on the Holy Eucharist.

As the congregation was praying the Rosary, I became acutely aware of how hot and humid it was in there. The church was not air-conditioned, but there were fans—only tonight with such a large crowd, they were little more than psychological encouragement.

Soaked in sweat, I was trying not to think about how uncomfortable I was, trying to concentrate on the rosary—when the Lord spoke to me: *I do not want you to preach on the Eucharist tonight.*

Lord?

Preach on my mother—on the Immaculate Conception.

Instead of following her example and saying simply, yes, Lord, I argued. It didn't make sense to preach on Mary! These people were Messengers of Mary; undoubtedly they already knew as much about her as I could tell them. Besides, it was not my style: when I went to people who were very Marian, I gave them something about the Holy Spirit. When I went to Spirit-filled people, I gave them something on Mary. I always went the other way—

Will you preach tonight, as I have asked?

Yes, Lord.

I gave my entire talk on the Immaculate Conception, about an hour and fifteen minutes' worth. When I finished, I was startled when the congregation rose to its feet, applauding. Had it been a Charismatic congregation, I would not have been so surprised. But this was a traditional church; Marian churches never did such a thing!

After the Benediction was concluded, I was disrobing in the sacristy, when a lady in her late 20's knocked. "Father, may I speak to you for a moment?"

I nodded, and she came in. "I want you to know," she confided, "I didn't intend to be here tonight. I'm a born-again Christian Catholic. I left the Catholic Church many years ago, became a Baptist, and worshipped in a Baptist church. Recently, I was Spirit-filled and joined the Assembly of God. Tonight, I had intended to go to an A.A. meeting, but my Charismatic friends said, 'There's this Catholic priest going to preach, and we think he'll be interesting.' "

As she looked at me, her eyes filled. "I didn't really want to come, but I came. And I was amazed: you answered all my questions, old and new—and you gave me back my Mother." There were tears in both our eyes now, as she said, "I want you to know: as of this night, I am back in the Catholic Church. I've come home."

Thank you, Lord. Now I know why You had me preach tonight on Your Mother.

10

Mother of the Living

Not long ago, a Protestant friend of mine, who has spent most of his adult life committed to the Lord's service as I have, asked me about the Catholics' glorification of Mary—were not some of us overdoing it?

The best answer I ever heard on the subject of glorifying Mary came from Scott Hahn. A former Presbyterian minister on the faculty of a Presbyterian seminary, he is a convert to Catholicism, whose journey from anti-Catholicism to his new belief was so painful that when he now defends Catholicism, he does so with compassion and deep understanding—especially when challenged by some of his former brother clergy.

"Scott," they say, "we can see how you *could* defend the Sacraments. And we can even see how you *might* be able to defend the Papacy. But how can you possibly defend the Catholics' glorification of Mary? There are crowning services, and pictures, statues of her everywhere! There's no way you can defend that Biblically! And with your

Biblical knowledge and background, how could you possibly swallow that one?"

Instead of answering right away, he asks them a question: "Was Jesus an Orthodox Jew?"

"Well, of course."

"And as an Orthodox Jew, would He have obeyed the Commandments?"

"Obviously."

Scott rephrases the question: "There's no possibility that, as an Orthodox Jew, Jesus would have disobeyed the Commandments?"

"No—why do you ask?"

"He would have honored his Father and Mother?"

"Yes, of course!"

"Well," he says with a smile, "in Hebrew, the word *honor* is *glorify*. So—He must not only have glorified his Father, but if He was a true Hebrew, He would have had to glorify His Mother, as well. So how can the Catholic Church be wrong in imitating Christ?"

And so, I told my Protestant friend, the Church does give glory to Mary, because she was the new Eve who said *yes* to God.

Writing more than 1500 years ago, St. Augustine observed that *Eva*, Latin for Eve, when reversed was *Ave*, Latin for Hail—the first word out of the angel's mouth, when he addressed Mary. (Luke 1:28) Eva said no, but Mary says yes to the angel's "Ave."

But as Killian McDonnell, perhaps our most prominent Marian theologian, is fond of saying: "Mary is one hundred per cent human, zero per cent divine." She is not a goddess, and while we may honor her and glorify her, we do not worship her or adore her. She merely reflects the glory of Christ, as the moon does the sun. By day, the sun gives all the light and warmth and power; by night, the moonlight which bathes the earth does not originate with the moon; whatever light the moon receives, it reflects earthward. And so Mary, in all her glory, merely reflects the far greater glory of Jesus Christ, her Son.

One place where my Protestant friend had no disagreement was that, of all mere mortals, Mary throughout her life was the one perfect example of obedience. And obedience—the voluntary choosing of God's will and way over one's own—was the human trait most pleasing to Him. *If you love me, obey my commandments. . .*

Jesus knew how difficult obedience was; He Himself, in human form, had sweat drops of blood in His struggle to put down His will, for the will of His Father. That was the hardest choice any man ever had to make—and being also God made it even harder: for He knew *exactly* what awaited Him—each lash, each blow, each nail. Each insult, each humiliation, each denial.

He also knew that at any moment He could call down a legion of angels and be instantly released from His agony. *Nevertheless, not my will but thy will be done. . . .*

Only one other human was ever able to say "yes" always—the one who gave birth to God the Son. Being totally human, she was not omniscient, but she was wise. She knew exactly what her obedience would cost—shame, ostracism, a life that would never be like her friends'.

But as daunting as her choice of God's will was at the beginning, it was even more so, at the end. She had enjoyed the company of her Son for thirty-three years. She had nurtured Him as an infant, was there at His presentation at the Temple, trained Him in the way that He should go (knowing, as no one else did, who He was and why He had come). She rejoiced as others came to know Him,

too—as first dozens, then hundreds and thousands of hearts
were drawn to the heart of God, by the example of His
surrendered heart. But none of these knew Him as she
did, as only a mother could, and with each passing year,
she loved Him more.

And then she was asked to give Him up, to be crucified.
Peter, the rock on whom He would build His Church, at
first could not accept the coming fate of his Master. But
she could. Though her heart was breaking, she silently
released Him to do the will of His Father. She was His
mother; of them all, it would have been hardest for Him
to say no to her. Had she spoken a single word. . . but
she refused to add to His anguish.

That was her greatest obedience. Yet she never thought
of herself as great; in fact, seldom, if ever, did she think
of herself at all. Someone else, playing such a key role
in the formation of the Early Church, might have been
tempted to pride. For she had been present at so many
crucial moments: she raised the curtain on His public
ministry at the wedding feast at Cana. She was among the
women who were always in the background as He traveled
and taught, who wept behind Him, as He labored up the
Via Dolorosa. And with John, she was at the foot of the
Cross, while her Son died.

Fifty days later, on the day that the Early Church was
born, she was praying in the Upper Room with the other
faithful, when her Son kept His promise and sent His Holy
Spirit to fill and empower them. The difference was, she
had already received the Spirit, at the time of the
Annunciation (which the angel acknowledged: "Hail, Mary,
full of grace"—Luke 1:28). So, not only was she praying
with them, she was undoubtedly praying for them.

As an archeology major studying in Rome in the early

sixties, it was my great privilege to be a member of the team that was excavating the Catacombs, where the earliest Christians actually were. The Early Church, in fact, specifically the first three centuries of Christianity, was the focus of my degree. I was present on that day in 1964, when a brand new part of the Catacombs was opened. There on the wall, we were awed to discover the oldest picture of Mary—and it was believed to have been done by Luke the Apostle.

Even there, at the beginning, the Church honored her— as it has ever since.

But her position, her role—her calling—never affected her. In her own eyes, she was nothing—a truth of which the Holy Spirit reminded me, when I once grew angry at Catholics who disregarded her.

One evening, at a prayer group to which I had been invited, someone mentioned the Blessed Mother. Immediately, someone else said: "Don't bring her in here! We don't need Mary here; she's nothing."

I got up and said, "If you don't need the Mother of God here, you don't need a priest of God, either," and I walked out.

The next morning, as I was with the sisters saying Mass, they sang a translation of the Magnificat which I'd not heard before: instead of singing, "He looked upon me in my meekness," they sang, "He looked upon me in my nothingness." In that instant, the Holy Spirit showed me that I need not be concerned when others said she was nothing; she had said the same thing herself.

Yet God the Father had chosen this nothing person, of all the women on earth, to be the mother of God the Son. . . . And He did not command her, He asked her. Through the angel, He said, in effect: will you be My mother? Extraordinary—no matter how much the Church honors Mary, it cannot begin to honor her, as God Himself did.

So, to perfect obedience, we may add the example of perfect humility. Meekness is the right word—and only a fool would equate that word with weakness. For meekness—the sum of all our choices for selfless obedience—requires more strength of character, more courage, than any other heroic act. Because it is usually accomplished in private, almost always goes unsung, and is invariably misunderstood. (What an encouragement it is, that the ones like Mary shall inherit the earth!)

Confronted by Mary's meekness, all my Protestant friend can do is nod. He is convicted, like me, of how far from her example is his own. But from her, he takes hope; if she can choose, so can he—and in his heart he gives thanks to God, for her. Which is where glorifying begins.

Be it done according to thy word—that was her fiat, and she is the model of everything we are called to be. She has been called the archetypical Christian, and I wholeheartedly concur: she is the archetype of the Church.

If in her first recorded words, she accepted God's momentous plan for her, her last recorded words, *Do whatever He tells you,* not only instruct the Church to obedience, they confirm what she has always done: directed attention to her Son. If the visionaries of Medjugorje are accurately reporting what she is telling them, then for eleven years she has been saying and doing the same thing: pointing people to her Son, and calling for them to be obedient to Him.

According to my Protestant friend, there is a common misconception among Evangelical Protestants that not only do we Catholics worship her, but we have put her in the place which rightfully belongs to her Son, and to Him *only*. Worse, some even say that if Medjugorje is authentic, then she has usurped His place!

It is difficult to remain dispassionate, when people who know so little about our faith, assume that they know so much. The temptation to put them straight, in equally condescending tones, is almost overwhelming.

But if you succumb, then whom do you serve? Not Jesus. Not His Holy Spirit, who is moving to unite the Body of Christ at the end of this age. The one who is served by your losing patience, is the same one who continues to foment the spirit of disunity. He could care less who is right, so long as both parties are convinced that the other is wrong.

As long as their eyes are on the Cross, their hearts are soft—and soft-hearted Christians constitute the greatest threat to his work. Because they depend totally on heaven, and they love one another—and that love draws countless uncommitted hearts to join them.

But if he can get their eyes off of their Saviour and onto their differences, then by adding his special seasoning of spiritual pride, jealousy, and vindictiveness, he can so harden those hearts that much, if not all, of their effectiveness for the Kingdom of God is neutralized. The recipe is potent; it has been dividing Christians for centuries.

Yet patience when one's faith is under attack—especially when the attacker's perception is totally skewed—is a virtue almost impossible to retain. God will help, if you will ask Him—He will grant you the grace to listen in silence. And

He will provide you with the right answer; He might even put it on the tip of your tongue.

One time, I was invited to be a guest on "The 700 Club," Pat Robertson's popular daily Charismatic television talk show. I was to be met at the airport, but when I got there and found no one, I just stood there, waiting. All the while, someone was paging a Brother Roberts to come to the desk. Finally, it occurred to me: I wonder if that's for me?

Just then, a young man came up and asked, "Brother Roberts?"

I smiled. "I'm Father Roberts, if that's who you want."

He nodded and explained: "Well, we can't call you Father; it's in Matthew: 'Call no man your father upon the earth' " (23:9). Inwardly I reacted to his absolute certainty of being right, and even more to the fact that I sensed it was a personal attack, although we had never met.

But I prayed for grace, and was smiling as I said, "Isn't that strange—what do you call the man married to your mother?"

"What do I call him? That's my father."

"What planet is he on?"

"That Scripture doesn't mean my actual father," the young man replied, as we walked out of the terminal, "it means anyone else."

"Does it say: call no priest, father? I think it says: call no *man.*"

"All right," he replied, "where does it say I *should* call a priest, father?"

"St. Paul did, referring to himself. In his first letter to the Corinthians, he said: "I am your father in Christ" (I Cor. 4:15).

As we drove over to the studio, we chatted amiably,

and finally he said, "You know, I used to be a Roman Catholic."

"Is that so?"

"Yes, but I found Jesus."

"Oh, really?" I smiled, unable to resist. "I hadn't realized we'd lost Him."

But there was no smile in response; this was a very serious young man. "The reason I left," he said, "is because you all worship Mary."

"You were a Roman Catholic—did you worship Mary?"

"I never did," he admitted, "but Catholics do."

I could now understand the edge—and possibly the underlying guilt—I had sensed in the beginning. It was too bad that when some people left a relationship or a marriage or a church—or a denomination—they felt that they had to tear it down, or make those who remained somehow terribly wrong, in order to feel better about having left.

Normally, I would not have pursued our conversation, but this young man was obviously spreading his poison to anyone who would listen. So I asked him: "When you were a Roman Catholic, did anyone ever tell you to worship Mary?"

"No."

"Did you ever hear of a priest bowing down before her and proclaiming her a goddess?"

"No."

"Ever hear of anyone praying: 'Almighty Mary —' "

"No."

"Well, then, where did you get the idea that we did?"

No answer.

He was hardly the only one to hold such misconceptions. As I traveled, I used to be amazed at how widespread they were. I am no longer surprised, but I am saddened—at how many committed Christians choose to believe the worst about other committed Christians, without a shred of firsthand evidence. Their delight in hearing bad news about others is almost as tragic as their delight in passing it on. Heaven only knows the harm that rumor-mongering has done to the Body of Christ over the centuries. As an abettor of disunity, it may rank second only to jealousy or self-righteousness.

Sometimes when I'm tired, or my nerves are a bit frayed, and some Protestant accuses Catholics of worshipping Mary and refuses to even listen to an explanation, I've been tempted to give him a taste of his own medicine: "You Evangelicals are so convinced you'll go to heaven no matter what, you feel that being born again gives you carte blanche to do whatever you feel like—from adultery to fornication to breaking just about every commandment in the Book." Which would be just about as stupid and abrasive as their accusing us of Mariolatry.

Incidentally, if in the wake of the recent televangelist scandals, any Catholics have harbored such opinions of Evangelicals, they might be interested in the response of my Protestant friend: he assures me that most of his friends (his committed Christian friends), do not have that attitude. While they know that they are saved by grace and grace alone, they also know that faith without works—without the life to back it up—is dead (James 2:17). They heed Paul's caution to the believers at Philippi: "Work out your own salvation with fear and trembling" (2:12). And they go by the old saying: "Face death, secure in your salvation; live daily, as if you might lose it at any moment."

Something else occurred on that visit to "The 700 Club" that pertains here. Someone, not vicious, not unfriendly, just curious, asked me: "How come you Catholics pray to saints—not just to Mary, but to a whole lot of them?"

I explained that under our interpretation of 'the Communion of Saints' which we all affirm every time we recite the Creed, saints have earned special roles in the afterlife, as intercessors. For us, the veil between the here and the hereafter seems quite a bit thinner than some other denominations suppose it to be.

"But if the door to the President's office is always open," persisted this one fellow, "why go to some assistant vice-president?"

I answered that question with another:

"Do you ever ask anyone to pray for you?"

"Sure, all the time."

"Why?"

"Because it's usually something for which I can use all the help I can get!"

"Exactly!"

"But I ask living friends to pray."

"So do we. To us, the saints are still alive—and frankly, we often need all the help we can get, too!"

He laughed. "Then you don't pray to Mary, instead of going directly to Jesus?"

I nodded. "I do go to Him, directly. And every time I say Mass or receive the Eucharist, I go to the Father, through the Son. But I will often ask Mary to come with me, to her Son. And she'll say, 'Yes, I will pray for you, and I will pray with you. But you do whatever He tells you.' Always, always, always, she sends you back to Him." I paused. "And if your prayer is answered, it will be He, not she, working the miracle."

The key to true ecumenism is in one's attitude. Obviously we cannot tolerate un-Christian behavior and belief. But we need not become pre-occupied with minor differences of emphasis. *By their fruit shall ye know them.* . . . Just as works and ministries can (and should) be judged by their fruit, so can individuals. And one of the first fruits is a person's attitude towards others not of his church or denomination.

Speaking of attitude, anyone familiar with Medjugorje can tell you that it is the attitude of that place—the spirit of Medjugorje—which endures and is so appealing. Consider what is reflected in the messages which the visionaries have long been receiving—compassion, humility, tolerance. . . .

Someone once asked a visionary to ask the Blessed Mother if everyone was supposed to become Catholic. To paraphrase her response: God was not concerned with what we called ourselves. He could examine our hearts; if they were turned toward His, that was basically what mattered to Him.

Another time, someone asked her through a visionary: who was the holiest person in the village? I smiled when I heard that; it reminded me of the disciples bickering over which of them would have the greater honor in the Master's Kingdom. The Blessed Mother's answer surprised everyone: she said it was a quiet Muslim woman (which gave certain Catholic theologians apoplexy, when they heard about it).

My Protestant friend tells of a Catholic priest (not me) who at the end of a long, good day together, said: "Look, why don't you convert? You know we're the one true Church, the only one which can trace its lineage straight back to Christ giving the keys to Peter. So, come home."

My Protestant friend shook his head. "Father," he said, "you and I both believe that the Bridegroom will be coming for the Bride *very* soon. When that happens, there's only going to be one Church, and it will probably be Catholic. Meanwhile, I'm still called to be an Episcopalian—but it will only be for a little while longer."

Attitude—tolerance or intolerance?

Those who enjoy their intolerance, do not reserve their prejudice for their fellow Christians: look what has been done to the Jews! And as with what has been done to Catholics, so much of it grows out of simple ignorance. If you don't *know* anything about a people, you are susceptible to being persuaded to believe just about anything about them.

I have heard of a rabbi who each Lent is invited to go to a different Christian church, to put on and explain a Passover Supper. As the people of that parish eat the lamb and the unleavened bread and the bitter herbs, he tells the story of Passover Night and the meaning of each sacred tradition. After learning a little of Jewish ways and breaking bread with one of their leaders, that congregation has a different attitude and a softer heart towards Jews.

Sometimes all it takes is for one to consider that we have a Jewish God. Our Lord Jesus Christ was a Jew. He was raised as an Orthodox Jew, with an Orthodox Jewish mother.

But bigots seem to reserve their worst venom for their own kind. It is beyond me, how some who claim to love the Lord, and are called by His name, can continually attack each other. I cannot imagine St. Paul saying, "I'm going to attack the church at Corinth today," or "those Christians in Rome—what a bunch a phoneys!" or "at least the believers in Galatia are real; they've got the Spirit!"

Nor are we Catholics immune: have you ever heard liberals and conservatives go at one another? Or those who prefer one devotion to another?

Ecumenism is not saying that it doesn't matter what you believe. It is not saying: we're all the same, just pick any religion you like, or mix and match and make up your own. Any religion perpetuating that kind of teaching would be promoting false ecumenism, leading to indifferentism and the lowest common denominator.

I am thoroughly Catholic and one hundred per cent loyal to the Pope, whom I believe is successor to Peter; I believe all that the Holy Catholic Church teaches infallibly and would willingly die for that faith. I also believe that watered-down faith leads to disloyalty and false ecumenism. But loving those who do not believe as we do, in spite of our differences, leads to true ecumenism.

True ecumenism is saying: "Hey, we all have some truth. We can come together in the Lord Jesus Christ, and we can proclaim that there is one Lord, one faith, one baptism, one Father of us all."

Division does not come from the Holy Spirit; it comes from the unholy spirit. What can you do about it? You can let the evil stop with you. The next time someone wants you to join them in running down someone else or some other ministry, don't do it. If the people they are condemning are doing something not of God, then, as Gamaliel reminded the Sanhedrin, they will fall soon enough (Acts 5:34).

And if you hear someone on the radio or TV, or before a group, say something like I heard recently: "The Roman Catholic Church is the whore of Babylon!" just remember: pray for grace. And unless you are awfully sure God is calling you to offer a rebuttal, do not give him or her back what they deserve. Only one person wins, if you get down in the gutter with them, and I'll give you a clue: it isn't Jesus Christ.

I have been asked if true ecumenism is even possible today. Not only is it possible, but it is vital and essential, right now. With the prophecies in Daniel and Revelation coming to pass—with Israel restored to her homeland, with the collapse of the old world order, and wars and rumors of wars everywhere—we no longer have the luxury of endless time stretching before us. The Holy Spirit is indeed preparing the Bride for the Bridegroom's return.

There may soon be a great shaking of the Church, leaving only a remnant of those who will not compromise their faith. But that remnant had better be united in spirit.

There has been that unity of spirit before. In 1977 in Kansas City, there was a Charismatic conference for all denominations. While the conference was staffed and organized by the Catholics (who had the most experience with large conferences), the steering committee was ecumenical, and at the conference virtually all the major denominations were represented.

All that long weekend, you could see the Holy Spirit drawing the different elements ever closer together, Messianic Jews with Classic Pentecostals, Lutherans with Catholics, Baptists with Presbyterians and Episcopalians. . . .

But it was not until Saturday evening, that He brought all present to their knees. Just at sunset, Ralph Martin received—and shared—a shattering prophetic word from God the Father. It gave His children a glimpse of what our division had done to His heart.

Mourn and weep,
  for the body of my Son is broken.
Mourn and weep,
  for the body of my Son is broken.
Come before me
  with broken hearts and contrite spirits,
  for the body of my Son is broken.
Come before me with sackcloth and ashes,
Come before me with tears and mourning,
  for the body of my Son is broken.

I would have made you one new man,
  but the body of my Son is broken.
I would have made you a light
  on a mountaintop,
A city glorious and splendorous
  that all the world would have seen,
  but the body of my Son is broken.

The light is dim, my people are scattered,
  the body of my Son is broken.
I gave all I had
  in the body and blood of my Son;
It spilled on the earth,
  the body of my Son is broken.

Turn from the sins of your fathers
  and walk in the ways of my Son.
Return to the plan of your Father,
Return to the purpose of your God;
  the body of my Son is broken.
Mourning and weeping,
  for the body of my Son is broken.

Stricken, many in tears, every one of the more than 40,000 people in that stadium got to their knees and begged God's forgiveness.

Then Father Mike Scanlan spoke and prayed a prayer of forgiveness, after which there was the greatest explosion of rejoicing that any present had ever seen! Up in the press box, a secular journalist from a local paper beheld it in awe, and likened it to how the Lord Himself would be greeted when He returned.

I share that now, as an encouragement. For while that show of unity has not recurred on such a large scale, the seeds for it have been planted. In a remote mountain village in Hercegovina, for eleven years the Mother of God has been calling men and women of all denominations to come (or come back) to God and restore the broken body of His Son.

11

Conversion

Behind St. James church in Medjugorje, along the footpath that heads through the fields towards Mt. Krizevac, stands a grove of cedars, in whose shade many of the villagers' parents, grandparents, and great-grandparents lie buried. It is an incredibly peaceful place—perhaps because so many prayers have been said there.

There can be twenty thousand pilgrims in Medjugorje—the services can be packed out, the summit of Podbrdo covered with kneeling figures. . . on Mt. Krizevac, each Station of the Cross can have groups clustered in front of it, praying in German or Spanish or Italian or English . . . there can be an endless waiting line at the church's gift shop and throngs milling in its plaza—but in the ancient cedar grove, there is always peace.

As you sit with your back against one of the cedars, the only sounds you hear are the murmuring of the cicadas, a sighing overhead as a breeze moves through the tops of the trees, and maybe the distant singing of an old "babushka" at work in the nearby vineyard. The air carries the fragrance of lilies—from a profusion of them growing by a grave-site in the southwest corner. In the warmth of the sun, you stretch and yawn, and examine one of the strange little pine cones, round and smooth like a marble.

And you smile: you can almost feel the tension of the long flight and bus-ride—and of all the days leading up to departure—ebbing away. You look up at the clear blue sky, and say, "Well, Lord, You finally have me here—now what?"

Or maybe you just say, "Now what?" Because 90% of the kids I bring to Medjugorje are not on speaking terms with the Lord—yet. Most of them come because they're curious—and that's about it. Maybe they've heard about Medjugorje from friends or at church; maybe their parents or a relative have urged them to go. Maybe they just want to see the sun spin, and the rosaries turning color.

Their motives may not be the worthiest, but I am not concerned about why they come. Time after time I have seen what God does, once they get there. There seems to be a special grace for conversion in that little mountain valley, so far removed from the world. . . .

And so, when we go out to that shady grove on the first day of a pilgrimage, one of the first things I talk about is conversion—the process that begins when one confronts the reality of God.

I do not push it at all; in due course, the Holy Spirit will move in each heart, in His own way and in His own time. And the way He touches each heart will be different— uniquely suited to that individual.

Were I to exert the slightest pressure, I could do inestimable damage to His time-table.

So it is a very low-key talk—little more than a gentle

preparation for the week to come. And as always, I answer questions. . . .

"Father Roberts, my aunt who's paying for my trip, hopes I'm going to get the message of Medjugorje—what's she talking about?"

For eleven years the Blessed Mother has been daily appearing in Medjugorje, to one or more of the visionaries, depending on which of them happens to be in the village at the time. Only four of the original six still see her every day; the other two are married now, and see her only on their birthdays or in times of great personal need.

Over the years, she has repeatedly called for five things: conversion, prayer, fasting, penance, and reconciliation. Taken together, these elements constitute the message of Medjugorje. It is not a message just for Catholics, or even Christians. She has made it clear that she has come for all mankind, to give them one more opportunity to turn to God.

Those who have already done this and are doing their best to live for Him, sometimes forget just how many people haven't. Once one knows that God is real, and that He cares deeply about each of His children, everything is changed. The world is totally different, as is one's place—and purpose—in it. There are new rules, new priorities, new opportunities—and a new, clean slate. Nothing will ever be the same again.

Their new God-centered world makes such perfect sense to them, it is difficult to remember that it makes no sense whatsoever, to anyone who has not stepped into it. All too often we assume everyone knows that God is real, and that they ought to be living for Him, even if they aren't.

But so many people who have not stepped into His Kingdom, look at us and think that we have completely lost our senses.

They do not see any reason why they should do the same—until they become aware of our inner peace, or quiet joy. Until they see our spontaneous unselfishness, our compassion, our cheerful serving and genuine caring for others. (It is not us they are seeing, of course; it is Jesus at work in us, but they don't know that.)

They begin to think that maybe, just maybe, we are not so crazy, after all. That maybe the lunatics *ought* to be running this asylum. . . .

Back home, there *are* hearts so surrendered that the Holy Spirit can use them as instruments to draw unrenewed hearts to the heart of God. But they are few and far between. In Medjugorje, where the Mother of God has been appearing in their midst so long and so lovingly, a great many hearts are surrendered to Him and desiring to become even more so.

As a result, there is such grace for conversion, that there may be no other place on earth where it is equaled. Into that environment, bring a mind that can be opened, a heart that can be softened, and just see what happens. . . .

That is why I bring so many young people to Medjugorje—as many and as often as I possibly can. My calling has many aspects—teacher, communicator, defender of the faith, encourager. But the part that is dearest to me (and, I suspect, dearest to Him) is ushering young hearts into His Kingdom. But not merely to become Christians; to become His totally surrendered servants— in religious vocations, or just as given, in lay vocations.

Whatever the reason (and in the end, it is a holy mystery and should remain one), nowhere else have I found ground so fertile for vocations as that in Medjugorje. In the little valley nestled in the Hercegovina mountains, it is rare that a young heart is *not* converted. The Holy Spirit seems to meet each one at precisely where he or she happens to be at that moment. If a young man has for years sought refuge from being hurt, in the strength of his superior intellect, he might be suddenly surprised by an act of surpassing supernatural love that defies rational explanation.

If a young girl has sensed a calling to enter a religious order, but her parents have discouraged her (amplifying her own reservations), she might find the Holy Spirit encouraging her spirit to be not afraid. She might discover that to lose all for the sake of Christ, is truly to gain all.

Whoever you are, wherever you are, there will He be. All your life, you may have thought that for better or worse, you were the master of your ship. And perhaps you were. But all your life, God has been waiting for you to realize that He is real, and that He loves you—beyond all human comprehension. Give Him seven days, and He will give you a new life.

He could do that, of course, in seven nanoseconds. But the Holy Spirit is a gentleman; He never forces Himself on anyone. And it often takes a full week for a closed heart to open—just barely enough to admit the possibility of God's existence. And that all of this might not be some spiritual Shangri-la—that it just might be real. And so might be the spiritual revival which has spread from here not only throughout the countryside, but all over the world, changing literally millions of lives.

But if it is real, then what of the so-called "real world"— to which we must return, at the end of our brief sojourn at the edge of heaven?

It is a beautiful thing to observe a heart slowly opening to God's love. It is like a rose, unfolding petal by petal in the warmth of the sun. When it is finally, fully open, it can receive the pollen of its new world—in the lightest touch of a butterfly pausing there.

It is difficult, of course, to leave it in God's hands. If the rose does not appear to be opening quickly enough, or looks like it may not open at all, let alone in time, one is tempted to take a hand in the process, move it along a bit. But that would be a disaster. When I was very little, my mother taught me to love roses—and never to touch them, when they were beginning to bloom. "That's God's part," she said. "You leave that to Him."

So I respect the fragility of each stage of the budding process. Nothing can undo God's handiwork faster than man's clumsy meddling. Young people are particularly sensitive to anyone attempting to manipulate them—so I keep a strict hands-off policy. But when they are ready to ask a question, I am ready to answer.

When broaching the subject of conversion, I make the point that this is the reason God has brought all of us here, including me.

"But Father Roberts, you've been a priest for twenty-five years; surely by now you're converted!"

If by that you mean: have I had an experience with God, asked Him to forgive my sins, and accepted him into my heart as Lord and Saviour? Then the answer is yes, of course—many years ago. It was sealed that night in Beirut, when I was filled with the Holy Spirit. From that moment on, I went to Mass daily, had a prayer life, read Scripture, and started cutting sin out of my life—all the things I should have been doing all along. I suppose that if I had to point to one moment at which my life changed, it would be then.

But that was only the beginning of my conversion.

For conversion, as it is understood in Medjugorje—and by all who have chosen the Way of the Cross down through the centuries—is an ongoing life-long process. The born-again experience, as my Protestant friend refers to it, is but the opening scene of a drama that continues until the moment of our death.

Conversion means turning everything over to God—not just one's will, but one's heart, mind, soul and being. The words that John the Baptist used to describe what must occur with the coming of the Master (John 3:30), apply to each of us inwardly, as well: "He must increase, but I must decrease." Bit by bit, self must diminish, to make room for the expansion of Christ within.

Now you can see why, for most of us, it does indeed take a whole lifetime! And I say "us," for no one—save Mary—has ever been exempted from the process. Another priest who has led a number of pilgrimages to Medjugorje, had always considered Marija the most spiritual of the visionaries. So he was startled one day, when she privately said to him: "Father, please pray for my conversion."

He was also convicted: for if *she* felt she needed prayer support in her struggle to surrender all aspects of her life to Christ, where did that leave *him*?

Conversion is a momentous challenge: ultimately, *everything* must be sanctified and made holy. Young people do not seem to be afraid of such a challenge—perhaps because they have not had as much time to grow accustomed to having life their own way. But you would be amazed at how we older ones, even priests, can equivocate and rationalize, when confronted with the need for conversion.

Because the process entails pain, when an area of self is nailed to the Cross, it is a shock to the system. The pain is acute and unavoidable. But if you will cooperate with the Holy Spirit, as He seeks to conform you ever more to the image of the Son, you will discover that the Cross is not a post but a door: you go *through* it, into the Resurrection Life with Christ.

In this age of spiritual anesthesia, pain—suffering of any sort—has become something to be avoided at all costs. But unfortunately, there is no painless way to sanctification. Nor did Jesus promise one: *If any man will come after me, let him deny himself, and take up his cross daily, and follow me* (Luke 9:23). That is why it is known as the Way of the Cross.

Of course, in His infinite mercy, He does not show us all at once, every area of our lives where further conversion is needed. Usually He does it one aspect at a time—and usually we already have a pretty good idea what it will be. In fact, we may have put off even praying about it (let alone dealing with it), because we do sense that what He may soon be requiring of us. (If, as you read this, your pulse is quickening slightly, you may relax; you've got three more chapters of grace time.)

When we are ready (which is not the same as when we *think* we are ready), He shows us what we must do. But it is only as much as we can deal with at that time, and He provides the grace (heaven's novocaine) to surrender what needs to go.

If it is a specific sin, like jealousy of a certain person, you may well be done with it, once and for all. But if jealousy happens to be at the core of your fallen nature, you may find that it is like layers of an onion—you peel one off, and are cleansed and forgiven and changed. But there will be other layers in the future.

The point is, do not be concerned about the future.

"Sufficient unto the day are the evils thereof " (Matt. 6:34). Be content to deal with only that which He is showing you today.

The shadows are lengthening; the sun is a fiery red ball on the rim of the mountains to the west. The bells of St. James are tolling. It is time to go there for the rosary and Evening Mass. In a little while, we will be kneeling in that place, and the Blessed Mother will be there, praying with us. And because she—and her Son, and Our Father, and His Spirit—are all more real to us now, we will be more able to do as she has asked, and pray with the heart.

12

Prayer

Last December, when the war raging in Croatia was expected to spill over into Bosnia-Hercegovina at any moment, Medjugorje was like a ghost town. Six months before, it would be difficult to find any time during the day when St. James did not have at least a dozen people in it, praying. Now the church was empty at high noon, as was the broad stone plaza in front of it. The restaurants and cafes were also vacant, though some were still decorated with bright pennants from early summer, when the main street bustled with pilgrims, and every available chair was taken.

Now the only sound was from those pennants, forlornly flapping in the breeze. Each shop still had one clerk in it, just in case a lone pilgrim might materialize, and enter in search of exactly the right rosary. But none ever did.

At dusk, random gunfire could be heard in the surrounding hills. Mostly it was harassment from the irregulars, meant to intimidate, or else it was some

Territorial Defenders, letting off a few rounds to break the tension. But everyone knew that in an instant it could escalate to total war.

Despite this (or perhaps in part because of it), Father Slavko Barbaric led a week-long retreat for nuns and friars, and one, a novice friar from America, went up on Podbrdo one afternoon to pray.

Previously, he might have had difficulty finding an unoccupied place to kneel, let alone collect himself in prayer. But now, the rocky, barren promontory with all the little crosses and the candle stubs was entirely deserted.

He knelt facing a tall, unadorned steel cross—a lone figure in a brown habit, kneeling on the rocks, limned in the late afternoon sun.

Somehow he seemed joined with all the other brown-robed ones who had knelt there and in other holy places over the centuries. Indeed, one could almost imagine the souls of all the friars who had been martyred in that land by Turks, Chetniks, Ustase, and Communists, kneeling there with him, as he kept his solitary vigil.

In places like that one, where the Blessed Mother first appeared and would still return on certain evenings when the young people's prayer group met there, prayer comes easily. You sense the presence of God—waiting. Prayer wells up inside of you and tumbles unbidden from your lips, like spring water. You could pray endlessly—and would, if that was pleasing to Him.

If you are an old hand at prayer, you have undoubtedly discovered other places where prayer comes that easily— old chapels or shrines or places of pilgrimage. Who is to say why? It may be that so many surrendered hearts make it easy for an arriving pilgrim to give his heart, as well. The heartfelt prayers of all those who have gone before, may have prepared the ground, so to speak.

In Medjugorje, so many people have prayed in so many places that the entire village and surrounding hills are unusually conducive to prayer. And there is always the grace—which rests on the whole valley like invisible mist. It has been said that prayer is the hardest habit to form and the easiest to break—but a newcomer finds him or herself falling into prayer quite naturally, just about anywhere.

When we talk about prayer during our gatherings in the cedar grove—and 95% of the Blessed Mother's messages deal with prayer—I start by having them listen to the silence. It makes them acutely uncomfortable, because they are so unaccustomed to it. Back home, there is always something playing in the background—a radio, a Walkman, the TV. Imagine eighty or ninety kids with nothing to listen to, but the breeze.

But if you do not have silence, you cannot pray.

So on their first full day in Medjugorje, all I have them do is be quiet. "I want you to hear God," I tell them. "I want you to see Him—really see the sky, the trees, the flowers. I want you to *listen*—so carefully and so sensitively that you are even aware of yourselves breathing." *Be still, and know that I am God.*

On the second day, I teach them the Lord's Prayer—not the way they usually say it, but the way Jesus taught it to the disciples: phrase by phrase. You can do this, of course, with any prayer, any hymn—giving it fresh and deep meaning by contemplating it, one word at a time. But it is especially effective with the Lord's Prayer.

I start by reading them Luke, Chapter 11, the first verse: "Now whilst He was in a certain place, praying, one of His disciples said, 'Lord, teach us to pray, just as John (the

Baptist) taught his disciples.' " I point out that they were all Jews, and it was part of the Orthodox Jewish faith to spend three hours a day in prayer. Those who were strict in their observance, like the Pharisees, might spend an hour praying the Psalms in the morning, another hour in prayer at noontime, and another at sundown—all highly visible in their diligence. The disciples were not Pharisees, but they had plenty of experience saying prayers.

And that was the whole problem: they realized that they were just *saying* the prayers. What they wanted, though they could not articulate it, was for Jesus to teach them to pray with the heart (which is also the message of Medjugorje).

Since that was what He wanted for them, too, He gave them a very simple prayer, brief but all-inclusive and easy to remember—the most beautiful prayer ever written.

I have them contemplate the first word: *Our* Father. . . why not *My* Father? Is He not my personal Saviour, and my Lord? But if it began *My* Father, that would foster a very self-centered attitude in my relationship with Him. Our Father reminds us that He is everyone else's, as well. He is also the Father of that black man, that Mexican, that Pole, that Indian. . . . And since He is their Father, too, then that makes us brothers and sisters. And it makes all who are called by His name, *our* family. . . . That word *Our*, with Father, instantly establishes both the vertical and horizontal aspects of our relationship with Him and with one another—the sum of the two Great Commandments.

I send them off for an hour to meditate on the Lord's Prayer, word by word. "Don't say the words out loud," I tell them, "*listen* to them.

And instead of you speaking to God; let God speak to you. Prayer is supposed to be a *two*-way dialogue."

I also remind them to go where they can be quiet. That

was what Jesus did: think how often we see Him going into the desert to pray, crossing a river to pray, going into the garden to pray, climbing a mountain to pray. . . .

Until I came to Medjugorje, I had never climbed a mountain to pray, never spent a whole night on one, in prayer; now I have done that several times—going up just before sunset, coming down at sunrise.

When their hour is up, they come back bubbling with enthusiasm. "Father Roberts, I couldn't finish! An hour wasn't enough time!"

I have to laugh at that, and I ask them: had someone a week ago suggested to them that they couldn't finish the Lord's Prayer in an hour, what would their reaction have been?

Now that they are beginning to experience what it means to pray with the heart, I emphasize that the key is to *listen* with the heart. All too often we get so engrossed in what we want to say to Him, we forget to listen for what He would say to us. He does not shout; when He speaks, it is in a voice so still and small, we must listen with all our faculties. It takes practice.

The floor is always open to questions, and as usual when we are talking about prayer, I get some doozies: "Father Roberts, God must be awfully busy, hearing and answering all the prayers from all the people praying at the same time. I mean, He only has one pair of ears, right?"

We have to be careful to let God be God, and not try to make Him in our image, when it was the other way around. And the fact that He made us in His image only means that we too, like Him, are spiritual.

If you work on a computer, you know that it can solve only one problem at a time. If it is a large or sophisticated computer, it may be able to perform several tasks at once, but its problem-solving capability is still linear—like ours. Now suppose it were infinitely powerful (omnipotent) and infinitely smart (omniscient) and plugged in to everything that was happening everywhere (omnipresent). With that capability, it could easily handle all problems simultaneously.

"But Father, they haven't even imagined such a computer!" Precisely. Just remember Who created Whom.

"Father Roberts, this is kind of dumb, but what exactly *is* prayer? I mean, are there different kinds?"

Prayer is thoughtful conversation with God the Father, or His Son, or His Spirit, or His mother, or the Saints— you really don't want to be talking to anyone else. It comes in three varieties: intercession, petition, and confession.

"I know this is going to sound selfish, Father, but I have a hard enough time praying for myself, let alone anyone else."

In praying for others, the secret is to pray for them, as you would have others pray for you—with interest, compassion, and perseverance. Remember, heaven's economy is perfect; "as ye sow, so shall ye reap" applies to prayer, too.

"How do I know who to pray for?"

Ask God. He will bring to mind whom He would have you pray for. And if you do not know what they need or how to pray, ask Him that, too. After awhile, you will have a regular prayer list, to which you will add and delete names.

"What about bigger things, Father?"

There are local, regional, national, and global concerns

that need prayer, as much as individuals do. Once again, ask God for inspiration. That word, incidentally, literally means His Spirit entering into a thing.

For eleven years, the Blessed Mother has been urging us to pray for peace, more than once reminding us that prayer can stop wars. It is ironic to recall that back in 1981, when she first made that appeal, there was no war—at least on the European continent. (Keep in mind that she was first addressing the local parish, Medjugorje.) With two evenly-balanced super-powers, peace was a necessity: the alternative was insanity, and they actually termed it Mutually Assured Destruction—MAD.

But look what has happened since 1981, as first thousands and then millions all over the world have been praying for peace, praying the rosary, praying with the heart: the Communist system has imploded. It has simply collapsed—voluntarily, peacefully voting itself out of existence. Coincidence? I think not. Mary herself said that when enough people were praying the rosary, Russia would be conquered. And in Medjugorje she has said that she would be glorified in Russia.

But into the vacuum left behind by Communism, rushed all the long-suppressed resentments and all the buried territorial ambitions . . . . Suddenly there *was* war, the worst Europe had seen in forty years.

The point is, the Blessed Mother had been calling for the Croatians to pray for peace—years before they would have any inkling why.

"So we should pray for the things God gives us, without knowing why?"

We should stop demanding an explanation, each time we are asked to do something. It's just rebellion—not wanting to be told what to do by anyone, even God.

Rebellion can be so subtle, we are not even aware of it. Indeed, one definition of it is: reserving the right to make the final decision. There may come a time, when your life will actually depend on your willingness to be instantly and unquestioningly obedient. That's the whole purpose of boot-camp; training soldiers to take orders. So that in combat, when the sergeant shouts: "Duck!" the private doesn't ask: "Why?" *Zing*.

Sometimes, intercessory prayer is that crucial. All of us have heard accounts like that of the man who was awakened in the middle of the night with a strong sense of peril and an urge to pray for a friend. He did, and after a few moments the urgency passed, and he went back to sleep. Later he learned that on the night in question, his friend had been on a plane approaching Tokyo Airport, when the pilot encountered a wind shear that almost caused him to lose control of the aircraft. . . .

"Father, I've been praying for a situation in a certain family for several weeks. I'm pretty sure God wanted me to start praying, but I haven't heard anything yet—how long do I have to keep praying?"

Until He releases you. Occasionally, He does let us know the difference that our intercession has made—but not very often, because faith is the essential ingredient in intercession. He gives us a prayer assignment—it may be no more than the fleeting notion that someone needs our prayers—and then sees how well we carry it out. The more we demonstrate our willingness to pray in obedience without knowing details, the more assignments He will give us.

You can see now, how intercession can become a real mission field. It is something that each of us should undertake each day, from the littlest child kneeling by the side of her bed, to her grandmother, perhaps bedridden, for whom intercessory prayer has become her main spiritual calling. "God bless Mommy and Daddy and Grandma. . . ."

"Father, when we're praying for ourselves, why don't we just ask the Lord to go ahead and make us like Him, and be done with it? You know, compassionate, humble. . . ."

It is better, believe me, to let God decide which aspect of your nature He wants to deal with—when, how, and to what degree. If you play God and decide which sin you would like to be done with—He might just grant your request.

My mother used to despair of my ego. "Son, when are you ever going to learn humility?"

"I'm working on it," I would quip—which shows how much I wasn't.

But one time, when I was going over to Medjugorje with quite a large contingent, five or six busloads, to do some TV shows for Heart of the Nation out of Hollywood, I sensed that my ego was warming up for an out-of-orbit trip. So with a friend and his wife, I prayed for humility.

The first afternoon we were there, since our group in their blue nylon jackets filled the church, Father Slavko invited me to give the daily talk to the English-speaking pilgrims. The camera crews were set up and waiting, and in the sacristy, after they made me up, the producers gave me a black satin jacket with very large, bright orange embroidered letters spelling out "Father Ken Roberts" and "TV Host."

As I came out into the sanctuary, our group, plus other Americans who recognized me now surged forward to greet me and get autographs, their flash cameras going off, as if I were some sort of movie star.

But down front and over to the left, there was one little old lady who was not smiling. Not at all. And when all the commotion had subsided, she walked up to me and let me know why, in no uncertain terms: "Sure, and what kind of a priest do ya call yourself?" she demanded in a thick Irish brogue. "Look at yourself! All dressed up like some kind of pumpkin!" Her words seemed to echo in the suddenly-silent church. "I never saw a priest act like that atall, atall!" And with that, she stalked out.

The talk and the taping went fine, but afterwards, having a coffee with my friends in a nearby cafe, I was still inwardly fuming. A pumpkin! I had never been called that in my life!

Noting that I was not my usual jovial self, my friend's wife suddenly burst out laughing.

"What's so funny?" I demanded.

"Well, you did pray for humility, didn't you? I think God just answered your prayer!"

Then I laughed, too: I had forgotten that a sure way to humility is through humiliation.

So—if you pray for strength, God may give you something heavy to lift. If you pray for strong faith, you may get more doubts, so that you can conquer them. And if you ask the Lord to crucify your ego, be sure to also ask for much grace!

· While confession is the last aspect of prayer I am covering here, it should be the first thing you take care of, in your daily quiet time with God. As you repent for the things you said or thought or did since your previous quiet time, and as He forgives you, your heart is made ready to pray for others and for yourself.

"What if I can't think of anything to be sorry for?"

Ask God. Ask Him to search any dark corners of your heart with the light of His truth, and show you if there is anything that needs confessing. There usually is.

You can begin to see how prayer can be more important in your life—important enough to merit a regular, defined quiet time.

"Okay, but when? If you knew what our house was like—"

Ask God. He knows your schedule—if you ask, He might suggest something that would never occur to you, like going to bed an hour earlier, in order to get up an hour early, to spend a quiet hour alone with him.

"But that last hour of the day is *my* time! That's when I finally get to all those things I've been trying all day to get to, and haven't had a chance!"

If an hour seems to be too much, start with half an hour. Or twenty minutes. The thing is to make a commitment and stick to it. That's the hard part, because guess who's going to come at you with any number of good reasons for quitting?

"Come on, Father, I can see maybe a few minutes. But *three* hours? I'd never make it!"

Time changes in the presence of God. Whereas in our daily life there never seems to be enough of it (and it seems like there's less and less all the time), when we are in His presence, we lose all sense of urgency. And when

His presence is strong, we forget about time entirely—in fact, we forget about everything else.

Sometimes young people who have not experienced that, ask me about heaven: they're afraid that it's going to be boring. "Standing around, singing and playing harps all day? Every day, for ever and ever? B-O-R-I-N-G!"

But then they come to Medjugorje and discover that God is real, and that He loves them, and it blows out all their circuits. "Father! That Adoration of the Blessed Sacrament last night was two hours long! I don't think I've ever been in church that long—but I didn't even notice! And you know what? I knelt up the whole time! *Unbelievable!*"

When we are close to God, time ceases. Eternity beckons—and it is not frightening. The more time we spend with Him, the more we want to spend—which is a good thing, because ultimately, we are called to pray without ceasing.

That may sound impossible, but it's not; it simply means to be living in a state of prayer. And if we are close to God, we will be.

"My problem is concentration, Father. I hate to say this, but until you had us spend that hour on the Lord's Prayer, I sometimes had trouble staying focused in prayer for three *minutes* at a time."

As I said, it takes practice. Start by admitting to God that you are having trouble praying and ask Him to help you. He will grant you extra grace and help you sustain your concentration. He may even suggest specific aspects of a concern to pray for, if you ask Him. But you've got to ask.

And remember: don't just pray the prayer, pray it with the heart. Take the rosary: if you will really take your time and meditate on each mystery, it will take on a whole new dimension.

As you concentrate on each mystery, put yourself in Mary's place: how did she feel? It's the difference between describing a rose, and experiencing the rose. I can describe the rose, its color, shape, size, and form. I can tell you what it smells like—but if I give you a rose, and you can smell it and feel it, you *know* that rose. Once you smell a genuine rose petal, the rose has shared its existence with you. It gave you its perfume, and now if someone says "rose," you can catch its scent again—that's concentration.

If I just think about the Annunciation, if I just think about what the angel said to Mary, and Mary said to the angel—that's surface-praying. But if in meditation I ask: Mary, how did you feel when the angel spoke to you? When he left? What did you feel at the Visitation? At the birth of our Lord? At His presentation? What did you feel when you lost Jesus, and then found Him? What was broken in your heart? Let my heart feel it, too.

In the sorrowful mysteries, I do the same for Jesus. What did you feel, Lord, in the Garden? What did you feel at the scourging? What did you feel, when they put the crown of thorns on your head, and spat in your face? When they jeered at you and mocked you? What did you feel, Jesus, when you carried the Cross to Calvary? What did you feel, when you were hanging on the Cross?

Many people tell me they have difficulty in meditating on the Glorious Mysteries, because the happenings are so phenomenal. I tell them to try to put themselves with the apostles and early Christians—to feel their excitement, when they witness the Resurrection. Feel the mingling of joy and loneliness during the Ascension, when Christ leaves them to await the coming of the Holy Spirit in the Upper Room. Then imagine the glory of Mary at the Assumption, when she is taken up, like her Son, and crowned Queen of Heaven!

I guarantee that if you will once pray the rosary all the way through that way, it will never be the same for you again.

On one of the first youth retreats I took to Medjugorje, I had 88 kids, and we all went to Kennedy Airport, to catch the flight over. When we got there, I said, "Now we're going to have Mass."

"Mass!" they exclaimed, "It's not even Sunday!"

"No, it isn't. But we're going to have Mass every day."

"Every day?!"

Eight days later, we were back in JFK. Our plane had been delayed—so much so, we missed our connection and were stranded for the night. Eighty-eight kids, sitting on their bags in the middle of the terminal, with no place to stay—and no one was the least bit troubled or unhappy. We just prayed the rosary together. The customs agent, other people passing by—they couldn't believe it, but all we felt was peace.

"But doesn't the rosary fall into the category of 'vain repetition'—the sort of mindless chant that Scripture warns us to avoid?" my Protestant friend once responded. "I mean, forget for a moment that it's all to Mary; isn't it awfully close to a Hindu or New Age mantra?"

Spoken like someone who has never prayed the rosary with his heart. First of all, if you really meditate on the mysteries, you will see that the entire focus is on the Gospel story—from the birth of Jesus, through His death and Resurrection. And I do not know of anyone who has done the full rosary without feeling closer to the Lord Jesus than before.

As for the repetition, it is not rote, if you keep your mind on Christ. The secret lies in the nature of your heart: if your heart is truly seeking the heart of God, then each decade will have meaning. But if it is not towards Him— if it is hardened in sin or your mind is elsewhere—then you can say a thousand decades perfectly, and your prayers will never get off the runway.

"Well, what are the advantages of saying the same prayer over and over?"

In spiritual warfare, a strong Jesus-centered, repeating prayer can be a tremendous weapon in the Christian's arsenal. For as the enemy skillfully seeks to confuse us and make us fearful, he can so distract us that we cannot pray at all, let alone effectively. It's like our mind has gone into fibrillation—which is the medical term for what happens to the heart, when it loses its regular beat and starts to flutter in panic. Emergency rooms are equipped with rubber discs which can administer an electric shock, to startle the heart and return it to its natural beat.

A repeating prayer like the rosary does the same thing for the mind—giving it a secure, trusted rhythm which gradually returns it to rationality. Think about the last time you were anxious or afraid and started saying the rosary— did you not feel the peace of Christ returning?

Satan hates the rosary, because it reminds the one praying it of Who will be the ultimate victor! To him, that prayer is a holy fragrance—it burns his nostrils and forces him to withdraw.

"Father Roberts, the Blessed Mother has asked us to pray for three hours a day; how are we ever going to do that? If you knew my schedule—I've got so much on my plate right now, I can't add another thing! And every bit of it is high-pressure stuff; in fact, right now I'm stressed to the max!"

When I hear that kind of reaction, I tell about a man with whom I spent some time last October. No one—*no one*—is under more pressure than he is. And yet his prayer life is the only thing that sustains him.

I was privileged to have a glimpse into that prayer life last fall, when I was in Rome with a group of mostly old friends, on a pilgrimage marking my Silver Jubilee, twenty-five years in the priesthood. Before the trip I had met a bishop from the Vatican who had said something like: "When you get to Rome, you must call me." Well, people say that sort of thing all the time—and often later wish they hadn't. So I did not take it seriously and somehow managed to misplace his number before we left. (When those who try to keep some semblance of order in my life read this, they are going to nod knowingly—I hope they are also smiling.)

On our last night in Rome, we had been out all day and did not get back to the hotel until midnight—only to find the concierge going crazy: "Father Roberts, where have you been? The Pope's secretary has called five times! You are to be at the Vatican tomorrow morning at 6:30, with vestments!"

That could only mean one thing: morning Mass with the Holy Father! The thing was, I had not brought any vestments with me—but because it was my Silver Jubilee, a friend had given me a new alb, just the day before. And another pilgrim, from Los Angeles, had given me a stole which she had made. That was when I realized that the following morning was a special gift from the Holy Spirit, for there was no way on earth I could have obtained a set of vestments between midnight and dawn. And they were brand-new, never used before.

Needless to say, I did not sleep much that night. In the morning, a couple of the men accompanied me to the Vatican, hoping that they might be admitted with me. We were half an hour early.

As we stood there, I had a moment of *deja vu:* twenty-five years before, right after my ordination, I had stood at this very door, waiting to have an audience with another Pope, Paul VI.

As the motto of my vocation, I had chosen Mary's response to God: *Be it done to me according to thy word* (Luke 1:38). And now, standing there, I realized just how much the opportunities of my priesthood had been arranged by Him, and how little I had to do with it. The books, the retreat and mission ministry, the television work—I had not sought any of those things, let alone merited them. All I could do was walk through the doors He opened for me—and then do my utmost not to disappoint Him. Now, I sensed, He was reminding me of this on my Silver Jubilee, by completing the circle in the way that He had begun it.

Finally the great bronze door swung open, and a Swiss Guard motioned me forward. The other two started to come with me, but he shook his head. "Just Father Roberts," he said.

I was shown to a waiting room, and because I was so early, it was empty. But not for long: in came the Bishop of Belleville, Illinois. "Ken! What are you doing here?"

"Same thing as you, I imagine, bishop." I replied.

The door opened again, and we were joined by the Bishop of Memphis, Tennessee, and then by the Superior General of this order and the Superior General of that one. . . . When the group was completed, there were twelve of us. Like the Lord's supper, I thought.

It was time to go. An officer of the Swiss Guard took us along the private corridors of the Vatican. As our footsteps echoed on the polished marble floor, I admired the great tapestries that few outsiders ever saw. The Bishop of Belleville, as awestruck and excited as I was, whispered to me: "How would you like to live in a museum, Ken?" I just shook my head in wonder.

Each time we would pass another hall, the Swiss Guard at the entrance would come to attention and salute. An elevator took us up to a floor where we were greeted by the valet of the Pope, in a tuxedo. He showed us in to the Papal apartments, into what seemed to be the Papal library, where we were asked now to vest.

As I was donning my new alb, the Pope's personal secretary came in and invited me to read the Gospel at the Mass. "In what language?" I asked.

"You will know that, when the book comes out."

Easy for him to say, I thought; he doesn't have to read it. Would it be Italian? Mine was awfully rusty. Latin? Even rustier. Polish? God forbid! No, Father, I'm sorry: be it done to me according to Thy word.

When we were ready, the doors opened, and we were shown into the private chapel of the Holy Father. I was surprised at how small it was; it could not have held more than fifty people. The altar was against the wall, and before it was a kneeler. The Holy Father was on it, sort of draped over it, deep in prayer.

Silently we were ushered to kneelers beside him. I was

on the third kneeler from him, and I could hear him groan, as if hearing a voice and responding to it. Whatever he was receiving was deeply troubling him; he would sigh and make an anguished motion—you could feel the agony of his prayer.

Tears came to my own eyes, and I sensed that all of us were similarly struck.

For half an hour we prayed with him in complete silence. Nobody moved, there was no rustling of vestments, nothing. Only the muted sounds of his travail.

Dear Lord, thank you for letting me be here. For letting me swear my allegiance to this man.

At 7:00, the clock struck. Two secretaries arrived; one Oriental, one Polish. They faced us, as they vested him for the Mass (I still did not know what language it was going to be in.)

It was time. Behind us were gathered the sisters who worked there and some of the embassy staff. All at once, the Holy Father turned and faced us and solemnly said: "In the name of the Father, the Son and the Holy Spirit." English!

It was like a dream, listening to the heavily-accented words, as he said the Mass. He spoke them slowly, as if meditating on each phrase.

When it came time for me to read the Gospel, about the man who had the devil cast out of him and who had to take care, lest seven worse, return, his eyes never left me. When I finished, I gave him the Book to kiss, and he returned it to the secretary.

I wondered if there would be a homily then, but instead, we knelt on in silence, reflecting on the Gospel message. Again, the Pope murmured to himself in prayer, shaking his head.

Now he began the prayers, his words were so slow and distinct, it was as if he had never said them before: "Almighty Father. . ."

It was one of those times where time itself seemed to slow—and I wished it would never end. I could listen to that heavy accent forever, because of the love he bore for each word, each act, of the Mass.

When it came to the consecration, from where I stood I could see his face, as he raised the Host. "This—is—My—Body. . . " And he just held it there, in adoration, his eyes shining. And then he knelt before the Host, with his forehead on the altar.

It was the same with the chalice—and I felt like we were in heaven, before the throne of God the Father Almighty. Others seemed to feel it, too; there were tears in all our eyes.

At the familiar endings of the closing prayers, where so many of us tended to rush a bit, our minds perhaps already on all that we had to do after the Mass, he took his time, praying with deep reverence, and as if he were reluctant to leave: "through our Lord Jesus Christ, who lives and reigns with You and the Holy Spirit."

We didn't leave. After he finished the Mass, he knelt again, in thanksgiving and adoration. And so did we—until we were silently ushered out.

I was amazed to find that it was after 9:00! We had been with him in his chapel for more than two hours—and it had seemed like less than half that long. Moreover, he had been at prayer before we arrived and after we left—and this was his daily routine!

We were shown back into the library, where we unvested, and were then taken to his private office. All the while, no one said anything; we were still enraptured by our experience.

Then the Holy Father came in, and when he came to me, he said with a smile: "And how is Mother Angelica?"

"Fine," I said with a laugh; someone had obviously briefed him.

We talked about my Jubilee year, and when I mentioned that we were on our way to Medjugorje, he nodded and smiled, saying, "Give them my blessing."

And then, for my Silver Jubilee, he gave me a special apostolic blessing.

That is the story I tell, when people say that the Blessed Mother is asking too much in her messages at Medjugorje, when she calls us to spend three hours a day with God.

13

Fasting & Penance

Up on the mountain, refreshed and renewed in spirit, and feeling close to God, it is easy to embrace the prospect of fasting. The Blessed Mother has asked us to fast on bread and water on Wednesdays and Fridays? *Nema problema,* as our Croatian friends say. We can handle that—it's only a couple of days a week.

But down in the valley—or more precisely, back in our own kitchens—it can be a bigger problem than we had supposed. Especially if we have never done any serious fasting before. Especially if no one else in our family feels at all inclined to join us. Especially if Medjugorje is already beginning to fade and take on the quality of a shimmering dream.

If you are determined not to lose what you gained in Medjugorje—or when the Holy Spirit first confirmed its reality to your spirit, without your ever having to go—then prayer and fasting together must become a regular part of your spiritual life. Just as they have been for saints, known and unknown, down through the centuries. And for the great prophets, long before the birth of Christ.

"Father Roberts, I can see the prayer thing, sort of, but I really don't think I'm a fasting person. I mean, starving yourself on purpose, and not even to lose weight—weird!"

If you have never fasted before, I could tell you that it is not nearly as hard as the enemy would have you believe. I could tell you that God will honor your denying yourself for His sake, by giving you enough grace to make it almost painless. I could tell you that your spiritual awareness will be heightened and your discernment sharpened (which is often why the saints did it, as a means of purification and preparation). I could tell you that you will be astonished at the extra energy you will have. And for you, all of that may indeed come to pass.

But if I were to tell you the whole truth, then I would also have to tell you that it can be hard, that you may discover that your lust for food is far stronger than you ever imagined. That you may, in fact, find out just how much you really do—or do not—love God.

Jesus never said that the Way of the Cross would be easy. What He said was: *Follow Me.*

"But Father, why buy pain? I mean, if you've got something to eat, and you're hungry, why not eat it?"

When Jesus was fasting for forty days in the desert, preparing for His public ministry, the tempter, knowing how hungry he was, said something like that to Him: If you are the Son of God, why don't you command these stones be made bread?

Jesus answered by quoting Scripture to him: *Not in bread alone doth man live, but in every word that proceedeth from the mouth of God* (Deut. 8:3).

In other words, unless you are one of those whose god

is their belly (Phil. 3:19), a little self-denial for the sake of Christ will do you no great harm. The key is to do it for Him. If you are old enough, or have been through enough, then by now you have realized that there is no way to avoid suffering in this life. Therefore, as long as you are going to suffer anyway, you might as well do your suffering in Christ and for Him, rather than just doing it on your own.

"What kind of fast should I do, Father? I'd do the bread one, except that I'm allergic to yeast and wheat, too, for that matter."

Ask God. (That seems to be my answer to just about everything—and, of course, it is. But once you've got a prayer relationship with Him—a two-way prayer relationship—doesn't it make sense to simply ask Him about everything? Isn't that what He wants you to do? And doesn't He have the best answers?) Anyway, ask Him what sort of fast you should do. Obviously, if you have a yeast or wheat allergy, a bread fast would not be the best. He will show you exactly what is right for you—but you must ask.

"You got it, Father: bread and water it is. But is it okay to run the water through a coffee-maker first? Just kidding."

Actually, that's a good question: for some people, the fast should be to the letter. But for others, especially those with a tinge of self-righteousness, such legalism would probably do more harm than good. And conversely, there are those who would take that statement and use it to cut themselves as much slack as possible, diluting their fast, until it ceases to be a fast at all.

As always, the best thing is to leave it up to God. Be led by His Spirit, and do not take on more than He would give you; spiritual pride is the deadliest of all the deadly sins.

"Father, my aunt who's on this pilgrimage says she's going to fast from television! Is that dumb, or what?"

It's not dumb at all. In fact, do not be surprised if the Holy Spirit indicates that in addition to the bread fast (or in place of it, if it is impossible), He would have you give up something other than food. For some people, giving up TV—or rock music, or cigarettes, or (let Him fill in the blank)—would be a far greater sacrifice. (Now you can wince; you knew this chapter was coming!)

Once you are reasonably confident that you know where and how He would have you deny yourself, then you must make a commitment—one that you can keep. Better to undertake a small fast and be faithful to it, than take on one that impresses you and others but which will be unlikely to be kept.

You can always increase a modest fast—and as your spiritual muscles grow, you may be led to. But if you break a fast before its agreed-upon duration, you are breaking a promise to God—which is a little different than cheating on Weight-Watchers.

For that reason, a fast should not be undertaken lightly. It should be arrived at prayerfully and entered into solemnly.

"Okay, Father, give it to us straight: how hard is it really going to be, and when is it the worst—at the beginning or the end?"

The most difficult time of a fast usually comes *before* you begin—in the struggle leading up to the commitment. For when you fast, you are committing an act of spiritual warfare. You are no longer a non-combatant. And so, the enemy will do all that he can to dissuade you from making such a decision.

As long as you remained as you were, you were no

great threat to him. He could let you ripen on the tree, as it were, knowing that eventually he could collect you at his convenience, or allow you to simply fall into one of his baskets.

But once you start to fast and pray—once you start to live the messages of Medjugorje—then you become something else: a soldier of the Cross, an instrument of Light, which God may soon use to draw others to the Light. And the more faithful you are to God, the more dangerous you become to the enemy.

"Sounds pretty heavy, Father, this Way of the Cross stuff—is it worth it?"

Look at those who have been steadfastly trying to live the messages, the ones who cooperate with the Holy Spirit, as He seeks to conform them more to the image of the Son—are they changing? Becoming more tolerant and compassionate? Is it getting so you can begin to see Jesus in them? Do you want those changes in your own life?

That's why the enemy will do all within his power to convince you not to attempt a fast, not to deny yourself in the areas you know would be pleasing to God. Because if you do, and you are successful, or you overcome, then it is almost certain you will infect others.

In spiritual warfare, as in the physical kind, an astute military commander (and the enemy has been at this for centuries) knows that the best time to defeat an invading force is before they reach the shore. They are at their most vulnerable, when they are bobbing ashore in small craft, unprotected. Accurate gunnery can foil an assault right there.

"So we can expect a hard time, while we're making up our minds—what about after we start?"

If the invaders do reach shore, that's the next best time

to hit them: before they have a chance to dig in and establish a beachhead. And so, you do start fasting, you can expect the enemy to throw everything he's got at you, right after you begin: *Everyone else is going to be having steak and corn on the cob tonight; your husband has even agreed to barbecue. You know they're going to want your best potato salad. And afterwards, they're all going to want to go for ice-cream. . . wouldn't it be better to postpone until next week?*

"So the trick is to bear down, and really get into it, and then he'll leave you alone, right?"

For the most part, but he's never going to leave you completely alone. Remember, the enemy has been at this a long time. He will not throw all his forces at you right away. He always holds one division in reserve—for about two hours before the last or next-to-last meal.

You know, you have really done well on this fast—better than anyone expected, including you. And the grace has been, well, amazing—that's the only word for it. Amazing grace. Of course, it may be lifting a bit now, since you're so close to the end. Actually, you're really hungry (induces pangs), and more bread just isn't going to satisfy it.

What you need is a sliver of that cherry cheesecake on the second shelf, just below the cold baked beans. (It may take some of them, too). Don't worry about the fast; you've already proven what you set out to prove, that you could deny yourself, when no one—especially you—thought you could do it. So you've done it, girl! You've won! And you deserve a reward—you've earned it, go for it!

Looked at that way, one can have a little more sympathy for Eve, as the serpent points out the merits of a certain Golden Delicious.

"From what you're telling us, Father, I get the feeling this isn't going to be easy."

The thing to remember is that fasting is war. For the sake of Christ, you have declared war on your flesh, specifically on its demand to be gratified, when, where, and how it chooses. And because it is a spiritual battle, you have spiritual weapons at your disposal, of which you may not even have been aware. You know that you have prayer and grace. You also have the Blood which Christ shed for you and with which He bought and paid for your soul. When you are harassed by the enemy, you can remind him of that, and you can ask the Lord to cover your mind with His precious Blood. Then, in the name of Jesus, you can rebuke the devil, and he will flee from you.

I can tell you these things, but ultimately there will come a time (if it has not come already) when you will have to learn them yourself, by walking through them. No one can do it for you, but once you have done it, you will never forget. That is why God permits the enemy to harass us: He desires all His children to *know,* through firsthand experience, that in any spiritual contest Jesus is *always* victor (regardless of what Hollywood might promulgate).

"Father, I wish you'd picked some example other than cherry cheesecake; that's been my downfall—more than once."

If it looks like you are about to cave in, and even prayer doesn't seem to help, look around: see if there is not an escape hatch. Because He never allows us to be tempted beyond what we are able to withstand. Pray, resist the devil, plead the Blood of Jesus, and you will be victorious.

And then He may say: *Well done, good and faithful servant. And because you have pleased me in this small assignment, I have another, somewhat larger, for you. . . .*

If fasting is denying yourself for the glory of God, then doing penance is taking on something for the same purpose. As the two so often go together—indeed, are opposite sides of the same coin—I have joined them together in this chapter.

The most familiar penances are those assigned in the confessional. But in the spirit of the Blessed Mother's messages at Medjugorje, they take on a deeper and broader meaning. Penance should flow from repentance, and the word *repent* means literally to turn and go in the opposite direction—which is exactly what we want to do, when we are convicted of a sin. And if we really mean it, then our change of heart will be proven by our deeds, as the New Jerusalem Bible puts it (Acts 26:20).

Has the Holy Spirit confronted us with how monstrously selfish we've been? Then, like Scrooge discovering that it's still Christmas and not too late to turn and go in the opposite direction, we seek ways in which we can be truly selfless.

Have we long held someone in unforgiveness, and been convinced that we *must* forgive? After so long a silence, the right words are often difficult to speak. But sometimes words alone are not enough; sometimes we must do works meet for repentance. As St. James wrote: "Show me this faith of yours without deeds, then! It is by my deeds that I will show you my faith" (2:18).

"Father, are you saying that if I've done something that hurt someone, not only should I ask his forgiveness, I should do something to make amends?"

Quite possibly—but you must ask God. Let *Him* assign the penance. If you assign your own penance, then you are acting as God: you are trying to be your own atonement.

"Is penance, then, a way of paying for our sins? I mean, can you undo them?"

Not by penance alone, but the Sacrament of Penance or Reconciliation can. Penance is a personal sacrifice, but the Sacrament of Penance is Christ's sacrifice.

A word about guilt: contrary to current pop-psych pundits, guilt is healthy; without it, we would not repent. But it is healthy, only insofar as it leads to repentance (with which we will deal in the next chapter). If it does not lead there, if the wound, instead of being cleansed and disinfected, is allowed to fester, then it can develop into a serious condition, much harder to cure.

Because the underside of condemnation (and it doesn't matter if it was put on you by someone else; if you accept it, you own it) is spiritual pride. Does that surprise you? Think about it: what you're saying is, "I am worthless in the sight of God. Beyond redemption and deserving of nothing but misery and dreck on this earth, I am an affront to God and my fellow man. . . ."

That is not God speaking. That is entirely your assessment. And it is false. Because what you are really saying is: you are too great a sinner to be forgiven. Which makes God a liar. For His Word tells us that the Lord Jesus Christ came for sinners. He did not come for the righteous; He gave His life on the Cross, that sinners, like you and me, might be set free from exactly this sort of bondage.

There is a deeper, uglier layer to condemnation: it says, in effect, that regardless of whether He could forgive me, I cannot forgive myself. Which is the pinnacle of haughtiness: my standards are higher than God's. And since I have failed to live up to them, I condemn myself to perpetual wretchedness, deserving of nothing but misery and dreck on this earth, et cetera, et cetera, *ad nauseam*. (Incidentally, if we, when confronted with our sin, are horrified at who we are—it only shows who we thought we were.)

The trouble with reverse spiritual pride is that it is a dangerous mire; you can easily get stuck in it. Guilt for its own sake can even have a certain morbid fascination: I have known people who have labored under condemnation for literally years.

Perpetual unworthiness is a lie from the pit. It is a very effective lie, for it neutralizes a Christian totally, and many who might have done great service for the Lord have been thus immobilized. Think: who is the one who condemns? Not God. He is the one who forgives. It is Satan, the accuser of the brethren. It is he who would lock you into remorse and despair.

So if you have been wallowing around in the slough of despondency, convinced that it will ever be your lot, then it is time you climbed out of there. Ask God to forgive you and cleanse you with His blood. Though your sins be as scarlet, He will wash you in the Blood of the Lamb, whiter than snow.

And while you are at it, if you have never prayed the Sinner's Prayer, pray it now: *Lord Jesus Christ, I come to you as a sinner, and I ask you to forgive me for all my sins, known and unknown. I invite you to come into my life, and reign there as Lord and Master, forever. Amen.*

Evangelicals consider this prayer essential to being born again. For Catholics, it is an act of contrition. (It would be a perfect act of contrition, if they were perfectly sorry) and it should be followed by the Sacrament of confession.

Now, if a Protestant ever asks you if you ae saved or born-again, the answer is yes. (It was yes before—the moment you first understood the need for conversion, and began trying to live for Him, instead of for yourself. But it will make them happy. And do not ever make a distinction between being a Christian and a Catholic; if you are living for Him, you are both.)

It does not mean that you are not still a sinner. Though you fully intend to go and sin no more, if you are like the rest of us, you probably will. When you do, you will have to go back to Him again, and ask forgiveness again. But each time, you will leave a little more of self behind on the Cross, as you pass through it.

It is painful, this Way of the Cross. But it is infinitely worth it.

"Father, what about doing penance for others?"

Again, let God do the assigning. You may ask Him, and He may agree, but it must be from Him.

On a pilgrimage two years ago, the young people got very upset with me, about my smoking. They would remind me that the body was the temple of the Holy Spirit, and that as its steward, I was responsible, before God, for keeping it clean. (Now *there's* a switch!) They would grab the cigarette out of my mouth and stamp it out or take a whole pack and tear them up. The more they did that, the madder I got, and the more I smoked.

But several of them were really distraught. "We want you to go on living, Father Ken," one girl said, her voice breaking.

It wasn't that I hadn't tried to give them up. For several Lents I actually did—except that I didn't consider that Sundays counted. As they were feast days, one suspended one's Lenten discipline on Sundays. Actually Saturday at midnight. . . .

My excuse was that the few times I had seriously tried,

I had put on weight. Which was very unhealthy, too, I reasoned: what was the point of saving yourself from cancer, only to die of a heart attack! And everyone I knew who had quit, had gained lots and lots of pounds. So as long as you're going to be unhealthy, you might as well be unhealthy in a way that you enjoyed.

On our last night in Medjugorje, a large number of the kids, thinking I had already gone to bed, slipped out of the house, some with blankets under their arms. Hmm, better find out what's going on. I went out and intercepted them.

"We're going up on the mountain—to spend the night on Mt. Krizevac, Father. You know, praying and stuff."

Suddenly I noticed that they were all barefoot. Pointing at their feet, I asked, "Where are your shoes and socks?"

"We're not going to use them."

I shook my head. "We were just up there a few days ago, so you know how steep and rocky it is. It's going to be extremely painful."

They just looked at me.

"Why are you doing this?" I asked.

"We're doing it as a penance."

"For what?"

"For you, Father."

"For me!"

"Yes, so you'll give up smoking."

I didn't know what to say. "Well," I murmured, "that's very nice of you," and I turned and went indoors.

Feeling very guilty (healthy guilt), I went to my room, shut the door, and had a cigarette. And another, and another.

The next morning, as we were packing, one young girl couldn't get her shoes on. Her feet were all swollen and bloody. She said there were others, and I noticed a number of them were limping.

You would think that I would never touch a cigarette again. That the mere sight of one would make me gag. Not so. As Paul cautioned the Hebrew believers, sin did have its pleasure for a season (Heb. 11:25), and apparently that season for me had not ended.

Last year, when my Protestant friend said he'd had two good friends die of emphysema, and that my wheezing sounded exactly like theirs, I told him that story.

He was shocked. "How could you remember those bloody feet and go on smoking?"

"Well, by now they're healed," I quipped, but he did not laugh.

"I think that's one of the most incredible acts of love I've ever heard of," he mused. "It gives me a whole other perspective on penance."

His pensiveness made me pensive—and I quit—for awhile.

Anyone who has ever tried to quit smoking will understand. I have heard that of all addictive substances, nicotine is the hardest to be free of. I don't know if that is true, but I do know a former heroin addict who told me that giving up smoking was harder than giving up heroin.

The dilemma, of course, was that here I was, telling people that they should have mastery over their appetites, rather than allowing their appetites to have mastery over them. I was not practicing what I was preaching—so I preached on other things.

A few months later, when my Protestant friend learned I was smoking again, he said, "You know, I cannot get the thought of those young people's bloody feet out of my mind," he marveled. "They did that for you."

"Look," I snapped back, "if I need bloody feet to remind me of anything. I don't need theirs; I have the bloody feet of Christ!"

My friend said nothing. He didn't have to; the guilt was back.

Pretty soon, it got to the point where every time I encouraged young people to let Jesus be Lord in every aspect of their lives, I could not help thinking of the one place in my life where He was not Lord; Joe Camel was.

Finally, I could stand it no longer. I threw my last cigarette away. And have not had another.

That might change tomorrow. A recovering alcoholic learns many things about himself—hard realities that it is worth his life to hold onto. And the foremost is that he is never cured. He can go for months—or years—without a drink. But the moment he has one, it can trigger the instant return of the full addiction—at its worst level. The same is true of smoking.

I tell myself that, when I am tempted. And I still am— after a good meal, in the middle of a good conversation, before going on the air. . . . I even occasionally dream that I've *had* a cigarette, so that when I awake, the thought comes: well, I might as well have another. (Guess where that dream and that thought came from?)

But the Lord always provides the grace, and when necessary, an escape hatch: an urgent phone call, or other distraction.

Or sometimes He just reminds me of what those kids did—or of another pair of bloody feet, with a nail driven through them. For me.

14

Reconciliation and the Eucharist

In the summer of '88, a year before the outbreak of Croatia's war for independence, Medjugorje was teeming with pilgrims. In the plaza in front of St. James, you could hear a dozen different languages, and all afternoon, along the shaded east side of the church, priests in chairs heard confessions. Beside each chair was a sign indicating which language the priest spoke, while out in the sun, far enough away to give privacy, were lines of pilgrims, waiting their turn.

The following year, a row of outdoor confessionals was built, but I would never forget the sight of all those pilgrims from all over the world, waiting patiently in the humidity and broiling sun to be reconciled with God. It underscored the importance of the fifth part of the Blessed Mother's message from Medjugorje: her call for all to become reconciled, with God and man.

I had taken my turn on those chairs, hearing the confessions in many languages. It was a soul-stirring experience: not in a quarter-century in the priesthood had I witnessed such honesty and desire to be at one with God. "Father, it has been eighteen years since my last confession. . . ."

Just as there seems to be a special grace in Medjugorje for prayer and conversion, there also seems to be special grace for those who would be totally cleansed and forgiven. Sensing it, first-time pilgrims feel an urgency not to leave the village without taking advantage of it. So they will wait sometimes an hour or longer, to make a full confession.

"Father Roberts, I don't see the point of Confession. I mean, why go to a priest? If I need to, I can pray to Jesus."

When was the last time you *did* pray to Jesus? Because those who pray to Him regularly—who, under the conviction of the Holy Spirit, say, "Lord, Jesus, I am sorry for my sin"—allow the Good Shepherd to gather them into the sheepfold. They attend church regularly, and confession is part of their lives.

"But Father, if God already knows what sins we've committed, and can see in our hearts that we're genuinely sorry, how come we still have to go to Confession? Why can't we just ask Him to forgive us and let it go at that?"

Under some circumstances, that is all you can do, and it is enough. But whenever possible, you should also avail yourself of the Sacrament of Confession. God wants you to actually hear the words of repentance coming out of your mouth. It is one thing to ask Him to forgive you in the privacy of your heart; it is quite another to confess your sins to another mortal soul.

But not just any mortal soul—a servant of God, ordained

by Him and specially graced to receive confessions and pronounce absolution. And absolution is important: it is God's acknowledgement that you *are* forgiven—the perfect antidote against the poison of condemnation, of your refusing to forgive yourself.

"I'm sorry, Father, but I still don't see why it has to be to a man."

For the same reason that you go to a man for Baptism— or would you prefer to baptize yourself? Mother Church is a sacramental church, and as such, she administers her sacraments by one who has authority to do so in her name.

A Pentecostal minister once challenged me on a radio show: "Why do you act like God, claiming you can forgive sin? Only God can forgive sin!"

"Do you believe you can heal?" I asked.

"God heals through my hands—I am only an instrument of His healing power."

He understood, when I answered: "A priest is also an instrument of God's healing power, for at his words, by the power of the Holy Spirit, sins are forgiven—and not just forgiven but removed, which is what absolution means: 'to wash away.' On the day of His Resurrection, when Jesus appeared among His disciples, He charged them: 'Receive the Holy Spirit. If you forgive anyone's sins, they are forgiven' (John 20:23, NJB).

A priest is not only an absolver in Confession, he is also an instrument through which the Holy Spirit can offer direction. There are times when we are in such anguish that we could not hear God if He spoke to us in rolling thunder, let alone a still, small voice. But we can hear our confessor—we may not like what we hear, but we have no trouble hearing him. (And we had better be awfully certain that he is not speaking for God, before we choose to ignore it.)

"Father, did the Early Church require its members to go to Confession? Or was that the Later Church, 'improving' on the way it was originally done?"

You should be grateful that Confession is not the way it originally was! The Early Church required public confession. (How would you like to stand up in the middle of the congregation and tell everyone what you've done?) Then you did penance in sackcloth and ashes until the Great Easter Vigil, at which time the bishop absolved you, and you were re-admitted to the congregation. That was reconciliation in the Early Church. In the 6th Century the church changed that, because they considered it too harsh. Today, your privacy is respected.

"Father, I'll admit I feel better after confession, and I'm glad I've gone—so how come I have such a hard time getting there? A month goes by, two months—the next thing I know, it's been a year. By that time, I can't even remember most of the stuff I ought to have confessed."

Confession is like prayer—a habit that's awfully hard to pick up, and awfully easy to drop. It helps to remember who wants you to drop it: it isn't God. And it isn't your church or your pastor or your mother. It is the enemy who wants you to downgrade its priority, because it serves as a reminder of your accountability. If you are following Christ's banner, then you are a Soldier of the Cross, and any soldier who goes by the book is going to be more of a problem to the enemy, than one who makes up his own rules, as he goes along. And if a soldier knows that his performance is going to be regularly reviewed by the Commander-in-chief, his performance-level is going to be consistently higher.

Therefore, the enemy is going to run a myriad of excellent reasons at you—why you should skip Confession, or just postpone it a week (and another week and another week. . .) If he can break your obedience, he has won a significant victory—as much as if he can get you to break your fast. It may not seem significant to you, in terms of the "real world." But in the spiritual world, which in terms of eternity is more real than the tangible one, it is.

"Frankly, Father Roberts, I'm sick of hearing about obedience—what a drag!"

The Lord knows that obedience can be difficult, especially to an earthly authority. Especially if that authority is not exactly sympathetic. That is why His prophet Samuel said that obedience was better than sacrifice (I Sam. 15:22). Because obedience is often someone *else's* idea of what you should sacrifice.

But obedience is what He asks, and what He honors, and the harder it is, the more grace He provides for you to make the right choice. You say that you love Him— do you? *If you love me, keep my commandments* (John 14:15).

That is why the enemy is so anxious to have you come out from under divine authority. The more you do, the more you will hold earthly authority in low esteem. He even glamorizes the rebel, in the romantic image of the ruggedly independent loner, carving out his own world.

And rebellion can be so subtle we scarcely notice it. One definition of it is: *Reserving the right to make the final decision.* "Freedom of choice."

Samuel was blunt: he likened rebellion to the sin of witchcraft (I Sam. 15:23). Which makes sense, when you think about it: Rebellion was what brought the Morning Star's expulsion from heaven, and his vanity plate is still REBEL 1.

Confession, of course, is only part of the reconciliation process. Repentance is another part, and that, as we covered in the prayer chapter, should be part of your daily quiet time. It is when you review the previous 24 hours, asking God to show you what you did that you shouldn't have, and what you didn't do that you should have. (Don't get down on yourself in the process: the Apostle Paul had the same problem—and admitted it to the believers in Rome, so they would not get down on themselves.)

You can also use that time to take care of any old business that needs to be repented of, or any old hurts that may have surfaced. The main thing is to get completely right with God—*before* you go to Mass, so that when you partake of the Eucharist, it is with a cleansed and pure heart. When I was young, no one would think of going to Communion, unless they had first been to Confession.

Unfortunately, many of today's kids are not even aware of sin, so they don't believe that what they're doing may be wrong. That is probably the greatest spiritual problem facing the youth of today. Because if you don't believe what you're doing is wrong, how can you repent?

Everyone is born with a conscience, that intuitive sense that a certain action is wrong. But if children are not brought up under parental authority, if they are not raised under Biblical discipline, then eventually they will not stand for anyone crossing their will, not even God. Parents who cannot bear to cross their children or give them "tough love" when called for, who cannot bring themselves to set standards of behavior and then uphold them, are dooming their children to lives of misery.

Long before we know God, we can hear His still, small voice saying no. If we harden our hearts against that long enough, we deaden our conscience till we cease to hear it. And then we have a new religion: If it feels good, do it.

Feelings, by the way, are not sin. Young people have powerful feelings, especially in the area of lust. But just remember: lust begins in the mind, and there is enough grace available to make the right decision. There's an old Chinese proverb: just because a bird flies around your head, doesn't mean you have to let it make a nest in your hair.

The Apostle Paul summed it up in his second letter to the believers in Corinth. He knew the sort of thoughts the enemy ran into the minds of new believers, and he encouraged them to "bring every thought into captivity and obedience to Christ" (II Cor. 5:10, NJB). I always smile to imagine grabbing a lascivious thought by the scruff of the neck and marching it into the presence of Christ!

"Father Ken, the reason I don't go to Confession is because I don't have anything to confess!"

The Apostle John had something to say about that in his first letter to all who would follow Christ: "If we say we are free of sin, we deceive ourselves; the truth is not to be found in us. But if we confess our sins, He who is just can be trusted to forgive our sins and cleanse us from every wrong" (I John 1: 8,9, NAB).

John then says the same thing a slightly different way (like some modern preachers), to make sure they (we) get the point: "If we say we have never sinned, we make Him a liar, and His word will find no place in us" (I John 1:10). Pretty strong stuff—his words (God's words), not mine.

But then he moderates his tone, and offers the antidote: "I'm writing this to keep you from sin. But if anyone does sin, we have in the presence of the Father, Jesus Christ, our intercessor who is just. He gave Himself as an offering for our sin, and not for our sins only, but for the sins of the whole world" (I John 2:1,2).

"Is that what it means, Father Ken, when Jesus is referred to as the Paschal Lamb?"

In ancient times, when the Jews committed sin, they would pray to God to forgive them, and would then make sacrificial offerings at His altar, to atone for them. The perfect sacrifice was a lamb without spot or blemish. On the night before Moses was to lead the people of Israel out of Egypt, the Angel of Death was going to claim all the first-born sons of the Egyptians. God gave Moses specific instructions for the preparation of the Paschal lamb (Paschal, meaning pertaining to the Passover meal). If the Israelites were obedient, and these instructions were followed to the letter, then the death angel would pass over their households, leaving them undisturbed.

Each household was to take a spotless male lamb without blemish. The lamb was to be drained of its blood to the last drop. The members of the family were to be spiritually cleansed by the blood of the lamb, which would wash away their sins. And then they were to eat the body of the lamb, every morsel.

You can see now why Jesus is the Paschal Lamb, the perfect sacrifice, who offered His Body and Blood as atonement for our sin. In a sense, each time we partake of the Eucharist, we re-enact the Passover meal, as well as the Last Supper.

"What I hear you saying, Father, is that sin is not an abstract theological concept."

Sin is real. And so is the way out of it. Reconciliation— repentance, confession, and absolution—is the process, and the Eucharist is its seal. That is why our worship is centered on the Eucharist, and that is true everywhere, including Medjugorje: the visionary Marija once confided that as wonderful as her daily visits with the Blessed Mother are, if she ever had to choose between them and the Eucharist, she would choose the latter.

And the Blessed Mother would wholeheartedly agree. Ninety-five percent of her messages deal with the need for prayer, and she has said that the most powerful prayer in the world is the Mass. It is that powerful, because it is not you who is praying, it is Christ, in the invisible miracle which takes place when He becomes the Body and the Blood, Soul and Divinity.

"Hold it right there, Father: I know we're supposed to believe in transubstantiation, but I'm a Chemistry major—"

I was similarly challenged once, by a very bright young scholar. Skilled in the use of a microscope, he was sure that if you submitted the bread and wine to scrutiny before and after, you would find no change in their molecular structure. To his surprise, I agreed. Then I offered a counter-proposal: suppose I were to subject them to intense radiation, would he eat and drink them? No! Why not? Wouldn't their molecular structure be the same? He saw it, then.

But if the miracle of the Eucharist is difficult to accept today, imagine how hard it was in the beginning! John lived the longest of the Apostles—some reckon he may have lived a hundred years. In that time, he must have celebrated the Eucharist for seventy of those years—so it is not surprising that he speaks of it with such reverence. "Take this and eat; this is my Body. . . . Take this, all of you, and drink from it; this is the cup of my Blood—

the Blood of the new and everlasting Covenant, which will be shed for you and for many, for the forgiveness of sin" (Matt. 26:26-28).

In the sixth chapter of John's Gospel, he describes the reaction of many of Jesus' followers, when He first told them that they would drink of His blood and eat of His flesh. They were horrified! Understand, these were not Pharisees, not His enemies. These were disciples—men and women so taken with His teaching that they followed Him everywhere; for three days, they had hung on every word, accepting His teaching on everything, and hungry for more. They could not get enough of Jesus!

When He said, "I am the bread of life. No one who comes to me will ever hunger; no one who believes in me will ever thirst," they all nodded in approval.

But when He said, "In all truth I tell you, if you do not eat the flesh of the Son of man, and drink his blood, you have no life in you," they all shook their heads. "After this, many of his disciples went away and accompanied him no more" (John 6:66, NJB). Note: none of them assumed He was speaking metaphorically or symbolically. He had always told them the truth, and had always meant what He said. They had no reason to doubt Him now.

You can imagine how their turning away from Him, hurt Jesus.

But He knew it would happen: only those who were given to Him by the Father would have the faith to believe and to endure to the end. And so, if others cannot believe in the miracle of the Eucharist, take no mind; just because they don't believe, does not mean it isn't true.

"But Father, why *daily* Mass? Isn't there a danger of familiarity breeding contempt?"

Some theologians are of that opinion. They point to

the Early Church, which only re-enacted the Lord's Supper on the Lord's Day, in other words, once a week. They feel that to celebrate it more often than that, devalues its currency, so to speak.

But other theologians are of the opposite opinion: since some have done away with so many other formal devotions—Benediction and Adoration, Novena Prayers, the Stations of the Cross, and the Rosary—it is a good thing that we do have Mass every day.

To me, accepted tradition of the Church is like an oak: the Early Church plants an acorn which slowly grows and develops through the centuries—watered, fertilized, and pruned by the Holy Spirit. Periodically, reformers, dissatisfied with the tree, have gone back to the acorn and replanted it—growing another tree.

We need to realize that contained within the acorn is a development of doctrine that is not at first visible. The Early Church did not have liturgy, as we have it. They did not have the structure we have, nor the hierarchy, although they did have a hierarchy. They did not have a central government office like the Vatican, or some synod, or some presbyterial office. These things all developed. It does not mean they are bad; it simply means that the Church, guided by the Holy Spirit, has gradually adapted to meet the growing needs of Christendom.

There are some who say she is not adapting fast enough. They have their own agenda for the direction in which they would like to see her move. It may not be God's—and that is the great safety in the methodical, deliberate pace of the Church's development: there is ample opportunity for the Holy Spirit to correct any aberrant growth.

There are others who would like to go back to the acorn, but that is equally unfeasible: we are no longer living in the First Century. And looking back over the development of the oak, I don't think God has done too bad a job of directing it.

Concerning the Eucharist, the Early Church did not have the breadth and depth of understanding that would subsequently be revealed by the Holy Spirit. To go back on that accumulated revelation would be like a college graduate re-enrolling in grade school: what he learned there was not wrong, but it has since been greatly expanded upon and amplified by the Teacher (by which name the Holy Spirit is also known).

So the Eucharist is available on a daily basis, and there are those of us for whom it will never become 'familiar.'

Incidentally, my Protestant friend also cherishes the Eucharist—though there was a time when he did not. He had grown a bit weary of taking Holy Communion every day (some Episcopalians do that), and he asked the Lord why it was necessary.

He was given a picture (which he refused to dignify by calling it a vision). In it, there was an ancient city, like an empty movie set for some Roman epic. There were vast civic buildings with endless marble steps and tall columns— the perfect setting for great ceremonial occasions and triumphal processions. Only all the facades were tarnished and covered with grime and soot, as if being eaten away by exhaust fumes and pollution (not unlike modern Rome).

This, he was given to understand, was his mind.

All at once, a dark crimson tide came washing in from the sides, rushing through the streets, rising up the steps, and splashing up on the buildings, even to the rooftops. As quickly as it came, it receded. And behind, it left every facade, every marble column and every step, gleaming white, stain-free. The city was immaculate.

This, he was given to understand, was the Blood of Christ.

After that, he never missed Holy Communion if he could possibly help it.

Reconciliation results in the fulfillment of the first Great Commandment: Love the Lord your God with all your heart and mind and soul and being. The vertical aspect of your spiritual life is fully restored.

But there is a second part of that Great Commandment, and without this horizontal aspect, there is no Cross: Love your neighbor as yourself.

The reconciliation process is not complete, until man, reconciled with God, is also reconciled with his fellow man. Which means, if you have "ought against any," there is still work to be done. (Note: it is not a suggestion or a request; it is a commandment.)

Forgiving seems to be awfully hard for some of us. We so enjoy the role of the aggrieved victim that we don't want to give it up—even if it makes us feel better about all of life, in general. Because as long as we are the victim, we are in the right, and they (whoever "they" are) are in the wrong. And if we enjoy being right, and forgiving them would make them un-wrong, we're not about to do it.

Oh, we make a good show of it: we ask God to forgive our unforgiveness and change our hearts; we might even make a big thing of forgiving the perp (police shorthand for the perpetrator of a crime). But we don't forget. We remember exactly what they did to us and how and why, and we justify our detailed remembering by saying: well, we're called to be harmless as doves, not dumb as doves.

If we cannot forget, we have not forgiven. Not the way the Lord intends us to. Not the way He spelled out for us in His Prayer: forgive us, Lord, as we forgive others. Think for a moment how we would like Him to forgive us: so completely that our relationship is as if we had never committed the offense.

Are we willing to forgive others that completely?

If you can think of someone whom you have not forgiven that completely—and your heart is telling you right now that you must—then I'm afraid it is no longer optional, but mandatory.

"Father, I can't tell you in public what a certain relative did to my little sister. He says he knows the Lord now and is sorry from the bottom of his heart, and I believe him. But I just can't change the way I feel about him: the sooner he goes to be with the Lord, or wherever else, the better!"

There was a Dutch woman named Corrie ten Boom, whose father had a little watch shop in their home in the town of Haarlem. During the war, they hid many Jews to keep them from being sent to concentration camps, behind a wall, in a special hiding place (which would be the name of her book). Her father's apprentice betrayed them to the Gestapo, and the ten Boom family themselves were sent to concentration camps. Corrie and her beloved sister Betsy were shipped to Ravensbruck.

Her sister died in the camp, but miraculously Corrie survived, and went on to become an evangelist, leading thousands to a new relationship with Christ. In the years right after the war, much of her speaking was in Germany, and not surprisingly, it was often on the need for forgiveness.

One evening, after she had spoken at a church service

in Munich, a man came up to her, full of joy at learning
that Jesus had forgiven him and washed away his sins.
Now he wanted Corrie to forgive him, too, and reached
out his hand to take hers.

She stared at him, stunned. It was the guard from
Ravensbruck, who had stood at the shower room door!
Suddenly she was back there, with all the anger and hatred
welling up within her. Her arm hung stiffly at her side.

He looked at her, his eyes pleading, but her heart was
like stone.

She prayed. "Lord, I cannot forgive this man. There
is not a bit of love in my heart for him. But Lord, you
do have love for him. You died for him. So you are going
to have to give me some of yours."

With that, she was able to raise her hand and take his.
The moment she did, she felt an overwhelming love for
this stranger, who until that instant had been her mortal
enemy. God had answered her prayer.

There is one other example of difficult forgiveness,
before we close the chapter. It has to do with someone
closely linked with Medjugorje, Sister Janja Boras, who was
long assigned there, and more recently was vice-provincial
of her order in Mostar, the capital of Hercegovina.

The convent in which she lived was on a quiet, tree-
shaded street, about three hundred meters from the
cathedral. Last winter, even with the streets crawling with
Serbian irregulars and paramilitaries, Bosnia-Hercegovina
was still technically "neutral," and the life of these sisters
went on as it had for years. Each morning they would walk
to the cathedral for Mass, then go about their daily tasks—
six to the hospital as nurses, others to teaching school,
and so on.

At the end of February, their quiet life was shattered.

In a national referendum the people of Bosnia-Hercegovina voted overwhelmingly to follow Slovenia and Croatia into independence. But Serbia did not want to let them go, and the war which everyone had feared, now came upon them. (Anyone desiring a better understanding of this tragic conflict and why each generation awaits its moment to take revenge, should read *Medjugorje Under Siege*, published by Paraclete Press.)

Like Sarajevo, capital of Bosnia-Hercegovina, Mostar was marked for destruction, with churches, hospitals, and schools at the top of the gunners' list. Miraculously a few phones still worked in Mostar, and one was in the convent. Friends in America were able to keep in touch with Sister Janja, and they relayed faxes around the country, to keep those praying, updated.

All through April and into May, the bombardment continued, reducing street after street to rubble, moving ever closer to the cathedral and the convent. Gradually the ferocity of the shelling increased, until the sisters were virtually living in the convent's basement, unable to go upstairs, much less risk going outside for food.

Two days passed, then three. One by one the houses on their street were being blown up, until the convent was the only one left unscathed. To assist the gunners on the surrounding hilltops, from the roofs of two tall buildings nearby, searchlights were focused on the roof of the convent. The heavy shells came closer. The house across the street from them received a direct hit at its front door.

In the basement of the convent, Sister Janja sounded very weak. She had gone without sleep for four days, and could not even remember when she had last eaten. Though she did not say so, both she and the friend with whom she was speaking, expected that her ordeal would end that night.

What she did say was: "Please thank everyone for their prayers. They are all that sustain us. But now I would ask that you pray for me this: if I am to die, pray that it be with only love in my heart for those who are doing this. Most times, I can keep love there, but it is getting harder—" and then her line was cut.

Sister Janja did not die that night. Miraculously she and the other sisters survived, though their convent was severely damaged. But when it seemed certain that she was about to go to the Lord, her only concern was that her forgiveness be total.

In the face of that example, can ours be any less?

15

Medjugorje Now

If you have never been to the annual convention of the Christian Booksellers Association, it is a gala event. Dozens of publishers present their new fall titles, while several hundred manufacturers proudly display the latest look in T-Shirts, wall plaques, banners, refrigerator magnets, and so on. (Books account for less than 40% of the revenue of the average Christian bookstore.) To this fair come several thousand bookstore owners from all over the country, to do their buying for the Christmas season and take advantage of the show specials.

Last July, it was in Orlando, and I went there on behalf of my previous book, *Pray it Again, Sam*. A tall fellow introduced himself as David Manuel, and aware of my relationship with Medjugorje, he informed me that he had just finished working with Father Svet on *Pilgrimage* and had caught the last PanAm flight out of Dubrovnik.

I told him that I had recently shared a platform with Father Svet at a Medjugorje conference in Wichita. There had been some talk of the Bishop of Mostar's opposition to the apparitions, and of the Franciscans' less-than-enthusiastic cooperation with his efforts to curtail them. At a press conference, a local reporter asked Father Svet: "When the Pope condemns Medjugorje, will you obey him?"

Svet speaks English well, but he seemed unaware that he was being set up. As he tried to explain that the priests at Medjugorje were only preaching the Gospel, I could see the press noting that he was not answering the question and unsheathing their knives.

To keep Svet out of next morning's headlines, I interjected: "Can I come in on this? Even though Father speaks English, he is not aware of the subtleties of the press. So I'd like to answer that for him, because he can't defend himself."

I looked at the reporter. "You are inferring by that question, that the Franciscans of Medjugorje are in disobedience. And I would like to answer that: I do not know more holy, more obedient, more loyal, more hard-working priests in the entire world, than the Franciscans of Medjugorje!"

The room was suddenly still. "The answer to your question is this: *If* the Pope condemns it, and you're making the supposition that he will, then, yes, they will obey." I paused. "As for your inference that they are being disobedient, if you had taken the trouble to inform yourself of the situation, you would know that the bishop is disobeying the Vatican. Because the case has been taken out of his hands—and that is the only instance I'm aware of in the history of the Church, that a local bishop has been relieved of all responsibility, concerning the authenticity of an apparition."

There was no response, only silence. "Because of his

prejudice," I went on, "the Vatican has taken the matter out of his hands and put it in the hands of the universal Church, turning the investigation over to a national council of bishops. Rome has also specifically directed the local bishop to stop harassing the visionaries, and to stop issuing pronouncements. But he has disobeyed every one of their directives.

So why not ask, instead: 'Why is the bishop not obeying Rome?' "

After the Wichita conference, we went down to Miami. Originally it was going to be a Medjugorje conference, but because of the hostility of some of the local priests, the bishop requested that it be called a Marian conference, instead.

The archbishop was there to greet the people, and he said that he was sure they were all disappointed to know that the Church had not approved Medjugorje. Only the way he said it, he insinuated that the Church had condemned Medjugorje, and a groan went up.

As the keynote speaker, I had an opportunity to respond to that, and I challenged anyone (as I do the reader now), to show me *anywhere* in the pronouncements of the Commission, where they said they condemned it. What their actual wording said was: "We cannot at this time *affirm* that it's supernatural." Smiling, I turned to the archbishop and said, "If I were to say: 'I cannot affirm that the archbishop here is speaking the truth,' I'm certainly not calling him a liar!" which got joyful applause.

I recalled some other reactions I had been encountering recently. Certain modern, up-to-date clergy were decidedly cool toward Medjugorje. They felt that its Marian aspect was non-ecumenical. Mary was out, finished; the Rosary was pre-Vatican II.

I asked them (politely, of course) what had they replaced her with? They had done away with the Rosary and all these other devotions—what had they put in their place? Were they studying Scriptures every day, and praying? Spending an hour a day in prayer with the Bible? No, they were too busy studying the new theories of modern theologians, attacking the Bible.

On one occasion, I was invited to speak on Medjugorje to a meeting of priests, about seventy-five of them.

It was a tough audience; they were peers, and I could see the cynicism on their faces.

I told them the story of the village and of how I came to be involved, emphasizing the Christ-centeredness of the worship. Other than the Ave Maria, all the hymns focused on Christ and the Eucharist, as did the prayers. Even the statue of Mary in the plaza in front of the church reflected this: neither of her hands pointed to her heart; they pointed away from herself. She was not drawing people to herself, as some had declared; she was pointing them to her Son. He was the message of Medjugorje; she was only the messenger.

I summed up with the truth: "I have been there many times, and I really think there is something supernatural happening there. It has brought me closer to why I became a priest in the first place."

During the question-and-answer period afterwards, one of the priests said: "Father, aren't you going to look stupid when this is condemned? You're going to have egg on your face."

"No, Father," I replied, "if the Church condemns Medjugorje, I will be an obedient priest and will never speak on it again. I will be hurt and sorrowful, but I won't have egg on my face, because I haven't lost anything. I haven't preached anything the Gospel doesn't preach. In fact, everything I'm preaching is what the Church is supposed to be preaching: conversion, Jesus Christ as Saviour and Lord, the need to read the Scriptures, because everything we need to know is in there, and that you must pray and fast for conversion and peace—which is also in the Bible. So if they condemn it, I won't have to change a thing I preach."

I waited, but there was no response. "I will have lost, inasmuch as I have made a mistake in believing it," I went on, "but I won't really have lost, because it has drawn me closer to God, and to the Eucharist, and has made me more prayerful."

I looked around the room at them. "On the other hand, suppose it isn't condemned? What if it is approved—and you haven't converted? Now, who's lost?"

After that, no one spoke for awhile. Then one asked: "Father, why do you take people to an unapproved place?"

"Well, Fatima wasn't approved for seventeen years and Lourdes eleven, but thank God people were going there before they were approved, or they might never have been approved!"

Another objection I ran into was one that was more likely to come from Evangelicals, like the man who called a radio show I had recently been on, right after the cover story in Life had come out. This caller maintained that Medjugorje was of the devil, that it was Satan, imitating Mary.

I asked him (politely, of course) if he was familiar with the third chapter of Mark? Then I refreshed his memory: when the scribes accused Jesus of casting out devils through the power of the prince of devils, He replied: "How can Satan drive out Satan? If a kingdom is divided against itself, that kingdom cannot last. And if a household is divided against itself, that household can never last. Now if Satan has rebelled against himself and is divided, he cannot last, either—it is the end of him" (Mark 3:24-26, NJB).

Throughout the messages of Medjugorje, Mary is repeatedly calling for people to turn to her Son and accept Him as their Lord and Master. She is warning them against Satan, who is prowling about like a roaring lion, seeking whom he may devour. It is showdown time now between her and the Serpent: the enmity that God put between them (Gen. 3:15) has never been spelled out more clearly!

I finished by drawing the caller's attention to the warning which Mark expressed in his very next words: Christ said that there was only one sin which could not be forgiven, in this world or the next. That was the sin one committed when one blasphemed against the Holy Spirit, by attributing to the devil what belonged to God.

And that is why the Church must be so cautious and its investigation of apparitions must be so exhaustive: it knows that the devil can impersonate apparitions. So how can we tell in the meantime? By the fruit. If I wanted to poison you, I wouldn't give you poison and mark it poison. I would put it in your favorite chocolate, especially if you're a chocoholic.

It might be 99% chocolate and only 1% arsenic—and what would the arsenic be? Something that was contrary to Scripture, something that was contrary to the teaching of the Church. An apparition might give you a lot of truth. But if there was one error slipped into that message, which was not of the Lord, that would be the arsenic.

"Did you ever find any arsenic?" David Manuel asked.
"Never."
"Were there ever any times that you had doubts?"

"Of course. But the Blessed Mother had a unique way of confirming Medjugorje to me—not only her presence there, but her call for me to continue leading pilgrimages there."

I told him then, about the three roses.

I didn't remember the first time I noticed it, but not long after I began speaking at Medjugorje conferences, three roses started appearing at significant times or places. One time I was giving a series of talks in Pennsylvania, traveling with friends in an RV from church to church. Based in Philadelphia, we were due in Harrisburg the next day, after giving three talks in three churches along the way. It was well into the afternoon by the time we arrived, and my friend who was driving said, "You know, Father, by the time you finish tonight, it's going to be ten o'clock, and the drive back to Philadelphia will take a good three hours. You're not going to eat until 1:00 A.M., if then. So you really ought to get something now."

I glanced at my watch: it was a little after 4:00 in the afternoon, an unusual time for a meal, but what he said made sense. So I agreed, and after driving around for awhile, we found a good restaurant not too far from the church. The maitre d' showed us to a table—there was a wide selection at that time of the afternoon—and we opened our menus, more hungry than we had realized.

In a moment the maitre d' reappeared, with a florist's arrangement. "Father Roberts?"

"Yes."

"These are for you."

There were three red roses. The card with them said: To Father Roberts from Mary.

I was stunned. When I could find my voice, I managed to ask, "When did these come?"

"Three o'clock."

"But—we didn't even know we were going to eat until 4:00." He stared at me. "And we didn't know where, until we saw this restaurant." Now there were goosebumps on all of our arms—and on David Manuel's, as I completed the story.

There was one more three-roses episode to go with it, like book-ends. Last year was my Silver Jubilee year, and so a friend had given me a silver rosary, with each bead a silver rose. One afternoon, on my last pilgrimage to Medjugorje, I was up on Apparition Hill, praying the rosary. While I was praying, one of the rose beads turned red, then another, and then a third. They have remained red to this day.

The final story in this book is the one which inspired it. It is another book-end (pun intended), balancing my introduction to Medjugorje, for it tells how my last doubt about Medjugorje was laid to rest.

I was traveling to England with a friend who had read *Playboy to Priest,* and was anxious to see my home town before my speaking schedule began. As we drove a rental car from the airport to Southampton, the closer we got, the more embarrassed I became: I hadn't a clue where any of my brothers and sisters, or nieces and nephews were. I had been out of England for more than twenty-five years, during which I had moved and they had moved, and I had completely lost touch. What was my friend going to think? Here was this priest who writes books and does TV shows, and has no idea where his family is—what kind of insensitive boor is this guy?

So—I prayed to Our Lady: "Mother Mary, I really believe you are appearing in Medjugorje, but I have to admit, there's about 10% of doubt left in my heart. Just to make me 100% certain, I want a little miracle. Not a big one—just find me one member of my family. Because I haven't got the faintest notion even where to begin looking."

When we arrived in Southampton, we went to the only place I knew for certain I would find someone I knew—the Redcote Convent. But it, too, had moved, and the extensive grounds had been turned into a subdivision.

Finally we located the convent, and, of course, all the sisters were quite old now, in their eighties and nineties. I was just going to visit and then leave, but their Mother Superior took me aside and asked me a favor. She told me of Sister Martha who was 97 now, and whom I remembered from my teen-age years at the Youth Hostel; she had been my mother's special prayer partner. She was in a coma now, and had been for two weeks. The hospital had released her, removing her life-support system and allowing her sisters to bring her home to her room, to die. Mother Superior asked if I would bless her and then stay the night and say Mass for her in the morning.

I agreed and blessed the frail old nun, so still in her bed. We slept in the priests' quarters that night, and in the morning, after I had finished Mass in the convent's chapel, a sister said, "Father, you're wanted on the phone."

Surprised because no one knew we were there, I picked up the receiver. A voice said, "Uncle Ken?"

"Who's this?"

"Your nephew, Nick."

I smiled, amazed. He had not been born, when I had left for America. "How did you know I was here?"

"Some lady called," he said off-handedly. "My mum is

down in the country, and I came by her place to check the mail and heard the phone ringing. So I let myself in, and this lady said, 'Your uncle is in town,' and she gave me this number."

I turned to the sister who told me of the call. "Did you, any of you, call my nephew?"

None of them had; they didn't even know his whereabouts.

So that was that; I stayed another day, to see my nephew and then my niece and that side of the family.

The next morning I had just finished vesting in the sacristy to say Mass, when Mother Superior hurried up to me: "Father! Sister Martha's regained consciousness!"

"What?"

"Yes! She's awake! Would you say Mass in her bedroom?"

So all the nuns were gathered around their sister's bed. Sister Martha was propped up on pillows; she was totally paralyzed and could not talk, but I could tell from her eyes that she recognized and remembered me—not surprising, considering all the prayers she had prayed with my mother over the years.

At Holy Communion, I took a tiny piece of the Host to her. A sister whispered that she couldn't swallow, had not had any nourishment in two weeks. With one hand I gently opened her mouth, and with the forefinger of my other hand, I placed the tiny piece of the Host, no bigger than a crumb, on her tongue.

Suddenly she grabbed my finger, and tears started to flow from the corners of her eyes. I gave her Holy Communion, my own eyes brimming, and throughout the service she clutched my hand, not letting go until the Mass was over, and I had to prize it away.

Back in the sacristy, I was removing my vestments when

Mother Superior knocked. "Sister Martha just died, Father," she said, her voice breaking. "You gave her, her last Communion."

I stayed to do the funeral, and because Sister Martha had helped so many teenagers in her long lifetime, it was well publicized. Everyone from my past life was at that funeral Mass! All my relatives, the nuns from other parts of England, and all the people from *Playboy to Priest*, including six ex-girlfriends—I had to laugh; Mary had gathered everybody from all over England for that funeral!

And I realized then, that even if I had been able to track them all down (which would have been a miracle in itself), I could never have seen them all, even if I'd had a year in which to do so!

I laughed again: I had asked her to find one person for me, to prove to me that she was appearing at Medjugorje, and she found—and brought—everybody!

I never doubted again.

Tears were in David Manuel's eyes, as I finished that story, and he looked around, hoping that no one in the bustle of CBA would notice. Then, ever the editor, he asked, "Have you ever written that down on paper?"

I shook my head.

"You want to do a book together?"

"Sure," I smiled. "I've read Wayne's; you did a good job." I paused. "Only we'll have to keep the focus on Medjugorje; otherwise, I'm obligated to my present publisher."

He smiled. "I wouldn't want it anywhere else."

So he joined me on a mission to Houston and on another to Baton Rouge, with the little red light on his ubiquitous tape recorder always on. And now you have read the result.

As of this writing (July, 1992), peace has returned to Medjugorje. The paramilitary oppressors have been driven steadily back, until they are now more than forty kilometers away. Electricity, phones, and water have just been restored to the village, and people are once again beginning to plan pilgrimages.

Access is a bit more complicated than before. The oppressors have also been driven from the hilltops surrounding Mostar, so the shelling there has ceased.

But the danger from snipers is still extreme, and down in Dubrovnik the fighting continues.

The way in is through Split. First you fly to Zurich or Vienna, then down to Zagreb on Croatian Air which has regular flights to Split, on the Adriatic coast. The bus trip from there to Medjugorje takes less than three hours. . . .

In Medjugorje itself, the church, the rectory, the sisters' retreat house, are all untouched; in fact, damage to the village has been so slight that it is a testimony to the prayers of the faithful all over the world. Doubly so, when one considers the testimony of a Yugo Army pilot who defected: they had been given orders to bomb Medjugorje, concentrating on the church, but when they flew over, they couldn't find it; it was as if someone had drawn a screen over the buildings.

Even if that were not so, even if the village had been obliterated and every person that we knew and loved there had been killed, they could not have killed Medjugorje. For it is no longer a place or a particular people. It is a spirit—a flame in the hearts of millions all over the world, growing brighter day by day.

Our Blessed Mother asks us to be more than messengers. She asks us to *live the message.*

She has given us the formula: convert, pray, fast, do penance, and be reconciled.

So we must ask ourselves: Is our heart truly given to total conversion? Does prayer, especially the Rosary, have a high priority in our daily life? Are we fasting? (Remember, a diet is a sacrifice we make to glorify ourselves; a fast is a sacrifice to glorify God.) What about penance? Are we denying ourselves the things or comforts which keep us from growing in holiness? And are we responding to the call to reconciliation? (Have we forgiven everyone who has ever hurt us? Do we regularly receive the Sacrament of Reconciliation to gain grace?)

Once we commit ourselves to *living* Our Lady's message, we discover a deep and lasting hunger for the celebration of the Eucharist . . . for that is where we commune with Him, where we experience His presence as in no other way—where we truly abide with Him, *up on the mountain!*